Omensford Series – Book 1

Bedsocks & Broomsticks

G Clatworthy

Foreword

A special thank you to my amazing typo hunters, grammar gurus, and plot pickers who got this story to where it is today. You are awesome!

If you want to support Gemma, you can find her on patreon for exclusive first reads of new stories. You can also join her newsletter for free stories at her website; www.gemmaclatworthy.com and follow Gemma on www.instagram.com/gemmaclatworthy, www.facebook.com/gemmaclatworthy or join the reader's group Gemma's book wyrms.

Chapter 1

"Have you tried turning it off and then on again?" Fi kept her face neutral as she watched the young man in a suit through the video chat.

"Of course I have!"

"Right, OK, let me have a look," her tone was blank, but she didn't believe him. Her power flickered under her skin. She forced it down. Her shift was nearly over, and she was not going to lose control today. She went through the standard checks then continued, "OK, this looks like a straightforward PICNIC error." Her lips quirked upwards at the use of her favourite acronym; Problem In Chair, Not In Computer.

"I'm going to force a restart and that should do the trick. Our connection will cut out, but you can call me straight back if that doesn't work."

The man on the other end of the call mumbled his thanks just before Fi disconnected the call. She let out a sigh and her mouse hovered over the next call in the queue. Just before she clicked it, an incoming call blared in the centre of her screen. She frowned at the picture of her boss's face. Normally he booked in meetings unless it was important. Probably more work for her to do or, maybe they'd announced the half-year bonus. She composed herself before she clicked on the picture and accepted the call.

"Fiona! Glad to see you."

"Hi Brian, what can I do for you?"

"Ah, well, I've got some news for you…" That was never good. She guessed her six-monthly bonus was going to be smaller than she thought. Probably due to the computers she'd accidentally destroyed. Fi listened to her boss on the screen as he droned through a pre-prepared speech about budgets and new directions for the company. She frowned, why tell her this? Was she not getting a bonus at all?

"…and so, I'm sure you can see that there are no other options. I'm very sorry we're letting you go."

Fi stared at the screen for a moment. Then she narrowed her eyes.

"I see. And who else is being 'let go', as you put it?" Fi wasn't quite able to stop the sarcasm edging into her voice.

"Er, well yes, at the moment it's only one role. The company feels it doesn't need a remote IT consultant any longer."

"Who's going to do my work, then?"

"Your calls will be divvied up around the rest of the team."

"So, if I understand correctly; I am the only one being made redundant." She took a deep breath. "But why? I'm the best consultant you've got. I even fixed the issue with the Davidson account when no one else could—"

Her boss held a hand up to interrupt Fi's protests, "Look we went through a fair process Fiona, we looked at past performance and cost to the company."

"Are you saying it's my fault the computers broke?"

"What I'm saying," her boss's voice was deliberately patient, "is that you're the only IT employee to need five replacement laptops and seven replacement phones in the last twelve months. You're also the only IT consultant who seems to have hardware issues thirty-three per cent of the time with your calls."

"So, you think it is my fault." Fi struggled to keep her breathing even as she felt the sparking energy build up inside her.

"I'm just looking at the figures here…"

"And there's no other options?"

"Well, we do have some roles in executive support or the in-house distribution centre."

"The post room?"

"If you're not interested in reasonable alternatives, then there really is no other option. Your mandatory severance pay will be in next month's payslip and–"

Fi didn't hear any more. Her magic surged, and the computer gave a small fizzle as the screen winked out. She swore. Another laptop bites the dust. She considered throwing the laptop across the room, but instead, took a deep breath and closed the lid before heading to the kitchen.

She defaulted to her normal method of calming her swirling emotions by baking up a batch of scones with a true crime podcast playing in the background. She threw the ingredients into a large bowl and began to mix by hand. After burning out several electronic mixers, she now stuck to wooden spoons for her baking.

It just wasn't fair, she thought, as she pounded the dough. Why did her magic have to be so inconsistent?

She was good with technology. Well, about fifty per cent of the time…The rest of the time, it had a habit of blowing up around her. But she was getting better.

She rolled the dough out and selected a circular cutter before viciously pressing it into the mixture. She slammed the baking tray into her small oven and set the timer.

She leaned on the wooden counter and took three deep breaths. Normally, cooking helped Fi to control her emotions. Not today. She clenched her fists and headed outside. Once she was far enough away from the house that her power wouldn't affect the electrics, she let loose with a frustrated scream. Sparking electricity looped from her body and crackled in the air. She directed it up into the sky and screamed again.

"Having a bad day?"

Fi opened her eyes and looked into the concerned honey-coloured eyes of her neighbour.

"Hi Glen, yes, er, I just got fired. Again."

"Sorry to hear that. I really thought they'd keep you on after you lasted the first six months." He looked at her sympathetically. This wasn't the first time the werewolf had caught her letting loose at the end of her extensive garden. Glen cocked his head and looked back towards their houses. "I don't want to be the bearer of more bad news, but I think your mother's coming up the path."

Fi let out a sigh. "Typical."

"I'll bring over one of Steve's comfort casseroles later."

"Thanks Glen, but there's really no need. See you later." Fi hurried inside. If she didn't answer the door, her mother would only let herself in. She opened the wooden door just as her mum was rummaging in her handbag for the key.

"About time! What kept you so long?" Nell stepped inside and made her way to the small kitchen. "Well, are you going to offer me a cup of tea?"

Fi rolled her eyes behind her mother's back and followed her into the kitchen. She filled the kettle and got out two mugs from the cupboard. She noted her mother's lips purse in disapproval and Fi allowed herself a small smile. Her mother had Standards. With a capital S. Tea should be made in a teapot and served in a teacup on a matching saucer. Fi took a perverse pleasure in deliberately making it in mismatched mugs.

"What's happened?"

Fi's shoulders tensed. "What do you mean?"

"Your hair is standing on end, and I can smell baking." Her mum's voice softened, "Come on, you can tell me."

Fi stirred the milk into the mug with tea in it before adding two sugars to her own cup of coffee and turning to face her mother. Better to get it out of the way sooner rather than later. She handed the tea to her mother and then took the fresh scones out of the oven and fumbled one onto a plate.

Nell opened her mouth, but Fi cut her off, "I just got fired." She hung her head as if she were a small child about to get a telling off.

"Again?! But I was so sure you'd keep your job this time, I mean, it's been eighteen months. That's the…"

"…Longest I've been at a company. Yes, I know Mum. But they tend to frown on things that cost them money, like going through five laptops in a year." She thought back to the meeting with her boss. "Make that six laptops. I'll get a new job, don't worry. They always need IT consultants."

"You're so good with technology…if only you could control your powers better when you get emotional…"

"Mum!"

"I don't blame you. It's my fault for asking the hotel to put in electricity, but I mean really it was the eighties and we were practically the only place in the UK without electrics. I never thought it would affect your powers."

Fi blinked. That was the closest her mum had come to an apology for anything. They both drank their hot drinks, and Fi savoured a rare mother-daughter bonding moment of quiet.

"You can always come back and live with me, you know." Her mum ruined the moment.

"No thanks! I can take care of myself," Fi tried not to notice the hurt in her mother's blue eyes. She changed the subject. "Why are you here, Mum?"

"I wanted to make sure everything was ready for the meeting tonight; you have done the slides?"

Fi sighed. Of course. The bloody Witches, Wizards and Warlocks Institute monthly meeting. Just what she needed tonight. No wallowing on the sofa watching brain dead TV and eating ice cream to commiserate yet another job loss. Fi took another bite of a warm scone. No, she was going to be pressing the forward button on a load of slides because none of the witches who were actually members could be bothered to do it, and her mum had volunteered her for the job. Bloody brilliant. They could all work a computer when they wanted to, just not when it came to pointless presentations for the WWWI.

"I've done the slides, Mum."

"And did you put in the photos like I asked?"

"Yes Mum, but it really is very simple to set up yourself, why don't I show you?"

Nell waved her away. "Oh no, I trust you, you're the expert with these things. Besides, it will give you something to do this evening instead of wallowing in self-pity."

Fi narrowed her eyes. Her mother didn't have psychic powers, or so she claimed, but that had been uncannily close to what Fi had been thinking. Self-pity and blowing up something in a violent computer game sounded just like what she needed. Fi took another bite of scone, barely tasting the buttery sweetness.

"Right, well, I'll be off then. Lots to do before the meeting and you'll be wanting to get on those job search websites. See you later."

Fi followed in her mother's wake as she swept through the hall and out the door. She considered slamming the door behind her mum but instead closed it with a sharp click. Bloody job websites. She felt the pressure of her power building and cursed as an arc of electricity shot from her fingers and blew the fuse of her hallway lamp. She stamped her way back to the kitchen, grabbed another scone, and cracked open a bottle of cold lager. Electricity crackled around her.

Chapter 2

"Burn the witch! Burn the witch!"

Agatha sighed and moved across the playground. "Now, now, children, that perpetuates hurtful stereotypes of both humans and witches. No one burns witches anymore. Come on, back inside!"

She clapped her hands together and shepherded the small band of supernaturals into the classroom.

"They used to though, Miss. My Mum says that there were witch hunters, and they would track witches, and catch them and then…"

"OK, thank you Huckleberry," a natural teacher, Agatha immediately launched into a question, "Since you're so keen on learning about witches today, who can list all the different types of witches there are?"

She repressed another sigh as Zadie's hand shot up, "And of course I'm using witch as the generic term for the class of magic user that includes witches, wizards and warlocks."

Zadie's hand slunk down. Agatha knew she should be grateful to have such a keen student in the rag tag supernatural studies class, but she couldn't help feeling as if the small girl had it in for her sometimes. She questioned everything. Not the usual things you'd expect from a seven-year-old like how to spell 'werewolf', no Zadie had that down pat.

She questioned the everyday things that everyone took for granted, like why supernatural beings hadn't assumed dominance over the mundane humans that shared the world. Agatha sometimes felt like Zadie was taking her for a ride with questions like that but the earnest expression in the child's brown eyes meant that the teacher couldn't just ignore the question and too frequently she felt herself falling back on the type of answers she hated giving her pupils. Really, 'because' just isn't a good answer. But sometimes it was all there was.

"I'll give you all a few minutes to think about it and write it down, then we can share with the class."

While the classroom filled with the busy sound of pens scratching over paper, Agatha's thoughts drifted to the WWWI meeting that evening. The Witches, Wizards and Warlocks Institute would be hammering out the details for the annual Tri Village Halloween Fete. The corners of her mouth lifted in a self-satisfied smile. Agatha knew she was in with a chance for the largest vegetable competition. She couldn't even practise the false modesty in her head. She was definitely going to win. Her pumpkin was so large it had taken up the entire greenhouse, crushing any opposition from the tomato plants that had attempted to annexe the sunniest spot. Secretly, she was worried that she was going to have to demolish the glass panelled building, but that was the price to be paid for the coveted prize of the largest vegetable in the Cotswolds. Turning her attention back to the class, she noticed that pens were slowing down over pieces of paper.

"OK, let's see what we've got then. Who's first?" Agatha ignored Zadie's waving hand and instead picked one of the less enthusiastic pupils.

Chapter 3

At exactly half past six, Fi's phone rang. She looked at the caller ID and sighed before answering. The lager had helped to mellow her and there was little danger of her power unleashing itself.

"Hi Mum."

"I was just making sure you are still coming tonight, and you haven't done anything stupid."

"I lost a job Mum, it's not like I'm not used to it. I wasn't going to kill myself."

"That's not what I was thinking!" Nell sounded shocked. "I thought you might have done something to your laptop."

"Ah." Of course. The bloody slides for the bloody WWWI. Fi briefly considered stamping on her laptop out of spite, but stopped herself. It was her own personal laptop and had survived many years of her power outbursts. Plus, she needed it for job searches.

"Fiona?"

"What? Oh, no, the slides are fine. I was going to set off soon."

"Good, I'm already here with Effie so turn up any time."

"The meeting doesn't start until seven and it's a ten-minute walk."

"Yes, so come over now and you can set up. Got to go, see you soon."

Fi glared at her phone and shoved it into her pocket. She shrugged on her beige trench coat and packed her laptop carefully into its leather carry case. It might be an old computer, but it had lasted, and she'd modified it over the years, so it kept running smoothly. She didn't want to risk replacing it unless she absolutely had to. Her modern work laptops didn't seem to last at all.

She pulled on her vintage converse trainers and grabbed her keys before heading out. She immediately regretted the coat. It was a muggy September night, with the sort of closeness in the air that preceded a storm. Fi began sweating as she headed up the shallow hill to the village hall. She crossed the road and noticed a door open. She swore and debated whether to continue walking when her niece spotted her.

"Aunty Fi!" The small girl bounded out of the house and across the length of the front garden.

Fi smiled, "Hi bumble Bea, how's my favourite niece?"

Bea shoved the gate open and launched herself at Fi for a hug. Fi patted Bea's back awkwardly, making sure that her powers were clamped down, then let her down quickly.

Agatha joined them and shooed her daughter back inside. Fi couldn't avoid her sister now. They'd have to walk together.

"Hello Aggy."

"Fi," Agatha seemed surprised to see her. She closed the low wrought iron gate carefully, making sure the bolt was latched so the chickens didn't get loose, and settled her hands into the pocket of her oversized hoody. "Where are you off to?"

"WWWI meeting, same as you."

Agatha let out a short laugh. "Mum roped you in as well, did she?"

Fi found her lips curving upwards. They weren't close, but they could always bond over their overbearing mother. Their strides automatically fell into sync as they moved forward together. They carried on in silence for several paces before Agatha spoke.

"Sorry about the job."

Fi sighed. News travelled fast in a small village. "Mum told you?" she asked.

"I saw Steve after school. He said he was baking you a casserole."

Fiona shrugged. Of course, Glen had told his partner about it and naturally, Steve had assumed that her sister would know. Their family was close. She couldn't be angry at him; he'd brought her the promised casserole, and it was delicious. As it always was.

"Layoffs, you know, the usual story," Fi kicked at a stone in her path and winced as it hit the tyre of a parked car.

Agatha laid a hand on her sister's arm, "If you need anything…"

Fi shrugged off the offer of help, "No thanks, I'm fine. I'll find something soon and it'll be fine."

"Mum would let you move back in you know; the house is way too big for her to look after by herself and I think she gets lonely sometimes."

Fi snorted, "No way. I am not moving back home, even if I have to sell my house."

Agatha pursed her lips and changed the subject. "My pumpkin's looking good, by the way."

Fi mentally kicked herself. She hadn't even asked after her sister's prized vegetable. But really. It was a pumpkin. What could she ask? "So, is it still in the greenhouse?"

"Yep, best place for me to make sure it gets consistent light and heat, although I've had to do a bit of enchanting to make sure it doesn't get too hot and over ripen. I don't want a mouldy pumpkin for the fete!"

"I thought enchanting was against the rules?"

"We-ell, enchanting the *vegetable* is strictly not allowed, but the environment is a different matter. I heard that Goody Winships over in Magewell has set up a magical watering system for her courgettes. Now as to plant feed…" Agatha was on her pet subject now and could go on for hours. Fiona breathed a sigh of relief as they arrived at the village hall. Yellow light pooled out of the doorway onto the paved path.

"I'd better get inside; Mum wants me to set up some slides."

"OK, see you later," Agatha let out her own sigh of relief and followed her sister inside.

Fi hurried to help Effie set up the chairs. She liked the elderly owner of the small café in the village, and had worked in the shop as a teenager, but the woman was ninety if she was a day, for goodness' sake. She shouldn't be lifting chairs, not even with her magic. Effie was, in fact, levitating a stack of five chairs precariously across the hall. The wooden folding chairs wobbled dangerously overhead before they unfolded and landed on the ancient wooden floor with a loud bump.

Effie muttered to herself as she turned to another stack of chairs. Fi placed a hand gently on the elderly lady's sequined cardigan.

"Why don't you let me help?"

"Oh, you're too kind, but I levitated much heavier things than spindly chairs when I was an undersea archaeologist in the Mediterranean."

Agatha joined them. "Not at all. We'd love to help. How are your hives, Effie?"

Fi rolled her eyes; her sister was unable to pass up an opportunity to help someone else.

The nonagenarian tilted her head to one side as if she was listening to something. "Oh, the bees have been a bit fractious lately, but they're almost ready for winter now. I think they'll have a little honey to spare this month, but I don't like to take too much this time of year in case there's an early frost."

"Well, they're always welcome in my garden." Agatha lowered her voice. "I've got an anti-frost spell over my tropical green house."

"Lovely dear, I'll let them know. Now, if you finish up with the chairs, I'll get the kettle on."

Fi left her sister to the chairs and set up her laptop on a rickety table. She didn't realise her mum was behind her until the witch spoke.

"And you're sure you included all the photos?"

"Yes Mum. It's all in there," Fi sighed. Luckily, more witches arrived and interrupted. Nell bustled off to greet them and most likely remind the lucky witches that they had agreed to help with something. Fi clicked a few buttons on the keyboard and stretched. All ready to go. She grabbed a chair from the semi-circle that Agatha was forming and settled herself as best she could against the uncomfortable wooden seat, determined to stay out of the meeting.

Chapter 4

The magical beings arrived slowly, trickling through the door of the village hall in dribs and drabs. At seven o'clock precisely, Nell seated herself in the centre chair behind a table at the front of the semi-circle. The chair legs scraped loudly against the floor. Nell smiled. She wanted all attention on her, the Chair of the Omensford branch of the Witches', Wizards' and Warlocks' Institute. She frowned a little as Effie, seated to her right, unwrapped a toffee sweet. The paper crackling in the expectant hush. Nell coughed and Effie beamed up at her before remembering she was taking minutes.

"Oh! We're ready, are we?" The ancient witch stuffed the toffee into her mouth and picked up a pen in her gnarled hands, topped with crimson nail varnish. She held the biro poised over a pad of cheap writing paper.

To the other side of Nell, Kathryn shook her head and pursed her lips in disapproval. Nell ignored the unspoken clash between Secretary and Treasurer.

"Welcome everyone to our September meeting of the Witches' Institute," Nell started. Kathryn coughed and stared meaningfully at Nell. "I mean the Witches', Wizards' and Warlocks' Institute, of course. So much longer, but so much more inclusive," Nell beamed round the room. It was a good turnout tonight. She was pleased with her initiative to invite other supernatural beings too. It fostered a good sense of community in the village and would look good on the next grant application.

"Before we get to Liv's exciting presentation on dream analysis," Nell nodded her head towards a witch in a pale suit who waved at the room. "I want to start with the main order of business..."

The double doors of the village hall creaked loudly as they opened. Nell glared at the new arrival, who dared to be late to her meeting. Steve's hazel eyes met hers sheepishly. The werewolf grinned.

"Sorry I'm late; I was just taking these out of the oven." The WWWI members oohed appreciatively as Steve opened a Tupperware container of chocolate cookies. He took one of the empty seats in the semi-circle of chairs and passed the container round. Effie flicked her fingers, and three cookies flew across the room to the head table.

"Thanks Effie." Kathryn took one and gave a rare smile. Effie frowned at the Treasurer. Nell reached for another and placed it delicately in front of her on her linen handkerchief. Effie took a pointed bite out of the remaining cookie.

Nell gave her secretary a look and rapped her gavel on the tabletop smartly to draw attention back to her. "As I was saying, our main order of business is the Tri Village Halloween Fete." Nell paused for dramatic emphasis, expecting something from her audience. A sea of faces blinked at her politely as they chewed Steve's biscuits. "As you know, Halloween is rapidly approaching and the sisters…and brothers of St Columba's WWWI branch have been on the phone. Unfortunately, they are no longer able to host this year's fete following a bus crash on their annual trip to Stonehenge."

Gasps came from around the room. Nell continued, "I have it on good authority that no one was seriously injured, but one of the warlocks decided to curse the car that rear-ended the bus and, well, it backfired. The warts are growing smaller by the day but understandably, they have other things to think about rather than organising the biggest event of the year…and of course I understand they lost the deposit on the coach, so their funds are rather tied. Naturally, when their Chairwoman called me, I was pleased to help and so…we will be hosting the Tri Village Halloween Fete!"

A murmur went round the room.

"Fi, the slides if you will."

Fi flicked the lens cap off the projector and aimed it at the hanging white curtains that covered the small stage at one end of the hall.

"Lights!" Nell commanded. She watched her daughter sway towards the light switch. She tsked under her breath as she realised Fi had been drinking. It was a small mercy she hadn't decided to use her powers on the lights, they were always more volatile when she'd had alcohol.

Fi pressed the light switch and plunged the room into darkness.

"As you remember from last year, Magewell swept the board in all categories…" the murmuring amped up a notch as Fi moved the slides forward showing pictures of the ribbon winners from last year. Omensford had placed second or third in most categories, but first place had always been just out of reach.

"It's that Goody Winships, she always cheats!" A voice came from the room.

"Now, now, that was never proved," Nell remonstrated.

"Don't mean it's not true," the voice insisted.

"Millicent Green! Please! I will not hear insults about another Chairwoman." Nell rapped her gavel again as Millicent continued muttering. Secretly she thought Goody Winships probably did cheat, but she couldn't allow that sort of talk to get back to Magewell.

"There's no way her brownies were better'n Steve's."

"Awww, thanks Milly." Steve blushed and smiled at the witch.

"Order! Order!" Nell shouted before remembering herself. She gave a small cough and brushed non-existent lint from her neat jacket, "All this means is that we will have to up our game as it were for this year, and we will be on home turf. So,

I want all entries sent into Kathryn toot suite. This year, Omensford will be the ones to beat, and we will take 'best trick in show' too!"

There was a burst of applause and a few shouts of "hear, hear" around the room.

Nell smiled. "Now, I have here a list of tasks that need doing. I have taken the liberty of assigning them out, but feel free to see me after if you feel you cannot contribute to the good of the village." Nell nodded to Kathryn, who passed out the neatly typed lists to everyone in the room.

"Toilets! Why'm I on bleeding toilets?!"

"Millicent please! You had those portaloos for the music festival on the farm in the summer…"

"Oh right, well, s'pose I can sort that then. But I ain't cleaning them."

"And I have a bit of news," Nell paused again expectantly, smiling across at her members, "Nicholas the mage is going to be opening the fete!"

"Oooo Nicolas Cage! I love him, how did you get him, Nell?" Effie cooed as she stopped scrawling the minutes.

"No, not Nicolas Cage, Nicholas the mage, you know, he's a member of the Wizards' High Council. He was on the news when there was that kerfuffle at Avebury. He's a local celebrity."

"I would." The witch to the other side of Steve nudged him in the ribs suggestively and snagged another cookie.

"And he will be accompanied by Madam Mim!" Nell beamed. An excited murmur spread through the room. Everyone had heard of Madam Mim; powerful sorcerer and purveyor of potions including the supernatural household staple *Cure All*.

A witch with greying hair made a sucking noise. "Shame it's not Nicolas Cage. I wanted to ask him about how they did the special effects on Face Off. He looked exactly like that other bloke."

Nell looked down at the elderly woman; sometimes she wasn't sure if certain witches pulling her leg.

"Anyway, now that's all sorted, over to you Liv…"

Chapter 5

Meanwhile, on the following Thursday, seventeen miles away in the slightly larger village of Magewell, Goody Winships brought her chapter of the WWWI to order.

"Ladies, please, if you could pay attention for a few minutes, then we can get to the dogs."

The members of the institute were already cooing over the puppies that the charity had brought in to demonstrate proper canine care, and, of course, try to rehome. By the looks of things, Petunia would be leaving tonight with all three of the cute dogs.

Goody Winships banged her gavel on the new table she was seated behind, trying to get attention back to her. In some ways, she was very similar to her old nemesis; Nell, not that she would admit to it. The members settled reluctantly into their seats.

"Please, I have an important announcement." She held up a piece of paper in her manicured hand to make her point. "I have been informed today that St Columba's will no longer be hosting the Halloween Fete." She paused to allow the murmurs to spread around the room. "Instead, Omensford will be hosting."

There wasn't quite the ripple of shock she was expecting but Goody carried on, "I know, I know, it's not what we wanted but clearly St Columba's were too intimidated by our success last year to come to us and so they have gone behind our back to Omensford."

"Let Omensford have the Halloween Fete, last year, it used all our contingency funding to pay for those marquees and having to sort out all the stalls and catering."

Goody Winships stared at Olga, her eyes boggling at the suggestion that this could be a good thing. Goody's wyrm, a small dragonlike creature, nestled around Goody's neck, opened her eyes and hissed at Olga.

Do you need me to help you teach her a lesson? Her familiar, Lady Cressida Charmington, spoke psychically to her owner. Goody was tempted, but instead she soothed the creature with a quick stroke along her spine.

"It will be alright, you'll still be able to enter and win all those prizes Goody Winships," Margaret, Goody's faithful number two piped up, smoothing over the troubled waters.

"Yes, thank you Margaret, that's the spirit." Goody tickled her pet's head soothingly, and the creature stopped hissing but kept her head raised and alert. "Yes, we will all be able to enter the competition categories of course. Margaret, take a note to confirm with the Omensford Institute what the categories will be this year. Of course, we'll completely understand if they need to reduce the number given the late notice that they are hosting." Goody Winships smiled to herself. That would rankle Nell Blair for sure.

"Not much point entering is there; you won most categories last year." Olga looked up from her knitting.

"Well, I must say that I did do rather well last year, it was quite unexpected, of course." Goody smiled as modestly as she could and patted her steel grey hair. "And if anyone would like any help with their entries, do let me know. Speaking of help, Margaret, take a note to offer Omensford whatever help they need to make this fete a success."

A bark stole Goody's attention away from the pleasant thought of Nell's face screwing up in rage at the offer of help. "And now, I'll hand over to Simon for his presentation on looking after dogs."

Goody sat back down and smoothed her plaid skirt. She was more of a reptile lover herself. Unfortunately, so was a large Labrador who bounded over to the haughty witch and slobbered over Cressida. The minutes of the meeting recorded the ensuing scuffle thus:

7:32pm – Priya (a member) took over the minutes from Margaret (Secretary) for the remainder of the meeting.

The wyrm was disentangled from the dog thanks to the efforts of Simon (guest) and Margaret (Secretary). In so doing, the Secretary obtained a large gash on her arm from the wyrm whereupon she was given a dose of Cure All (see accident record #15) and the Chairwoman advised her to "Pull herself together". Simon (guest) offered to drive Margaret (Secretary) to the walk-in clinic in Cirencester.

One of the dogs (cockapoo) jumped up at the Chairwoman and attempted to lick her face, knocking her to the ground (see accident record #16).

Chairwoman Winships stated that she hoped that Simon (guest) had proper insurance for his "mutts" and added that she "regretted the decision" to allow the animal charity to attend the meeting.

At which point, Olga (a member) suggested the policy of allowing supernatural pets to attend the WWWI to be discussed at the following meeting. Seconded by everyone present. Chairwoman Winships noted the motion and asked Margaret (Secretary) to add it to the forward agenda. The Secretary pointed out that she was unable to take notes due to her injured arm. Chairwoman Winships acknowledged this.

After being helped up from the floor, Chairwoman Winships requested that someone clean up the dog mess on the hall floor. Simon (guest) offered to pay the dry-cleaning bill for Chairwoman Winships skirt.

Chairwoman Winships declared the September meeting of the Magewell branch of the Witches, Wizards and Warlocks' Institute closed at 7:37pm.

Chapter 6

Agatha made her way upstairs slowly, careful not to tread on the creaky step halfway up the staircase. She looked in on her seven-year-old daughter, Beatrice. The small child was spread out on the bed, cuddling her favourite ratty old teddy bear with her covers lying in a pile on the floor. Agatha smiled and stepped inside the room to pick up the pink duvet and lay it over her daughter. She had just finished tucking Beatrice in when the doorbell rang.

She briefly considered ignoring it, but she had a feeling about who it might be and a witch learned to trust her intuition. In this case, Agatha's intuition told her that if she didn't answer the door, her mother would come in anyway. With a sigh, Agatha headed back downstairs, pulling her fluffy orange dressing gown around herself. She opened the door as quietly as she could.

"What are those?"

Agatha followed her mother's gaze to her feet. "Bedsocks."

Nell visibly shuddered and stepped inside, brushing a dusting of raindrops from her smart coat. "Why are you wearing such hideous clothing?"

Agatha flexed her foot, admiring the bright stripes that circled her socks. "They keep my feet warm."

"It's a wonder you have a husband. Anyway, I wanted to ask if you needed me to crochet you a cover for your pumpkin…in case of frost."

"There's no frost forecast Mum, I checked with Effie."

"Yes, well, I wouldn't put anything past those sneaky witches at Magewell to conjure one up."

"Mum! Please! They are not out to get us. This fete is meant to be a friendly affair to celebrate our magic and join with the other supernatural villages nearby."

Nell arched an eyebrow at her eldest daughter. "Of course. But that doesn't mean Goody Winships and her lot won't do anything underhand. Do you know she sent me a letter offering to help this year? She said she knew it would be difficult for us to pull something together on such short notice and offered to help to make it a success!"

Agatha frowned as she puzzled out her mother. "That sounds like a nice offer…"

"Yes, well, she thinks she can pull one over on me. I wrote back and said she could help with the toilets. That'll teach her!"

"Mum!"

"I don't suppose you know anything about this?" Nell could change course in a conversation faster than the small children she dealt with every day.

Agatha looked at the crumpled poster her mother thrust into her face. In fact, she had encouraged Liv to go big and bold in a small revenge against Nell's weekly WWWI meetings, which threatened to become daily as they approached the day of the fete. She struggled to keep a straight face. "What's wrong with it? You asked for eye-catching?"

"I did not ask for a Samhain Spooktacular!" Her mother shook the offending poster at Agatha. "We are dignified witches, and I am not catering to the commercialism of Halloween at our traditional fete! Look at this picture!"

Agatha glanced down at the silhouetted picture of a witch riding a broomstick against the backdrop of a full moon.

"It's bold…"

"It's brash! She'll have to redo it."

Agatha swallowed her snort and turned it into a cough. Her mother narrowed her eyes and peered at her.

"Are you alright?"

"Yes, fine," Agatha managed.

Nell took a breath and scrunched the paper into a tight ball. "And I am not going to let Goody Winships win! This year is our chance, I can feel it! We are going to sweep the board and that includes the largest vegetable. I'm counting on you! I'll pop by tomorrow with the cover. You can't be too careful.

Good night." With that, Nell opened the front door and headed out into the rain.

Agatha shook her head and shut the door. She locked it and considered conjuring a ward against interfering mothers before deciding it wouldn't do any good. She climbed the stairs, wincing as she forgot about the creaky step, and entered the calm of the master bedroom.

"Who was that?" Neville put down the biography he was reading in bed, carefully marking his place with a leather bookmark.

"Just Mum, she's worried that I'm not taking care of the pumpkin." Agatha listened to the rain lashing against the window and started brushing her hair. She looked down at her fluffy socks. "Do you think my socks are hideous?"

"I happen to find bedsocks very erotic…especially when they're all you're wearing."

Agatha smiled across at her husband and deliberately shed the rest of her clothes before climbing into their king-sized bed.

Outside their bedroom window, a flash of magic lit up the sky.

Chapter 7

Fi sat bolt upright with a yell. The alarm clock buzzed angrily next to her bed. She yawned. It had been a long night. Nell's flashes of magic had flared through the sky until past midnight and the sounds of angry words between the werewolves next door had floated through the walls, until she had heard one of them leave and head for her mum's Bed & Breakfast. She didn't know what passed between Nell and the werewolf, but the magic practice ended shortly after.

Fi rubbed the sleep from her eyes as she got dressed. It was early morning, well before sunrise. Her mother had insisted on everyone being ready in plenty of time so she could lord it over the other villages. And her sister was nervous about the vegetable competition, so was heading in early to make sure that she got a prime spot. The doorbell sounded. Right on time.

Fi yawned again and went to open it. Her sister was there in loose fitting tartan trousers and a plain knit top.

"Ready to go?" Agatha rocked back and forth on her heels.

"Just give me a minute," Fi turned and donned her trench coat over her black leggings and jersey dress. Agatha followed her inside.

"Had any luck on the job front?"

Fi winced, "Not yet."

The truth was that she'd looked at job sites for IT roles, but every time she moved to apply, a pit of dread had filled her stomach and stopped her from uploading her resume. Instead, she'd thrown herself into baking. Ostensibly, she'd done it after her mum had badgered her, but if she was honest, making scones was a welcome distraction from her job search.

"Look, I know we don't always see eye to eye, but I understand why you don't want to move back in with Mum, so I agreed with Neville…" Agatha dug in her pocket and pulled out a cheque.

Fi bit her lip as she stared at the amount. The money would really help. She only had enough savings for one more mortgage payment, and then she'd have to talk to the bank. But where would that leave her bid for independence? This wasn't the first time her sister had bailed her out, either. She shook her head reluctantly. "No, I can't. Thanks for the offer, but I'm fine. Something will come up."

Agatha shrugged and turned away. Fi pretended not to notice that her sister stuck the cheque under the empty fruit bowl. Her sister always wanted to help out, she liked being responsible for everyone and, despite her independent streak,

Fi had taken her hand outs before. She chewed her lip, at least she could wait a few days to make up her mind about paying the money in.

Fi put on a fake smile and stacked up the tins of scones as her sister turned back. Fi wobbled, trying to balance them in one hand while grabbing her keys and phone with the other. Agatha took three of the tins from her sister and helped carry them out to the dirty pick-up truck. Fi settled the tins in the back seat before climbing into the passenger seat.

"Where's Neville?"

"He's coming later with Bea. I didn't want to wake her this early."

Fi nodded in reply, wishing she was back in her warm bed or at least had thought of making a cup of coffee to bring with her. A strong, black coffee. With two sugars, she daydreamed, maybe even three sugars. Calories didn't count in daydreams. The sisters were quiet as Agatha drove the truck down the hill to the designated field. Agatha joined the queue of traffic to get into the site and drummed on the steering wheel impatiently.

"I can't believe so many people are here this early," Fi commented as she gazed at the cars of half the village waiting to get into the exhibitors' parking.

"Believe it! Mum was clear; be here early or you won't get a spot."

"What's that coach doing here?"

Agatha peered in the direction Fi was looking in and adjusted her glasses, "Mum's not going to be happy about that…it's the Magewell coach. They weren't meant to get here before eight…"

Fi watched as the coach ignored the signs and pulled up outside an adjacent field. Several witches and wizards piled out, each clutching boxes or tins that contained contributions to the various competitions that would be judged later that morning. She caught sight of her mother striding over as fast as she could in a tweed suit. Nell grasped her clipboard tightly; her lips pursed. A sure sign that someone was going to get a talking to. Fi was glad she wasn't in the firing line.

The queue of traffic slowly moved forward, and eventually they were in the field. The elderly warlock took one look at the giant pumpkin in the back of the truck and waved them along a dirt track that led directly to a large, white marquee. Some wag had put up a yellow traffic sign that declared 'Heavy Plant Crossing'. Looking at the huge marrow in the back of the convertible in front of them, Fi could see why.

Once they had parked up behind the marquee, there was still the problem of getting the pumpkin inside the tent. Fi and Agatha considered it from all sides.

"We could try to carry it in…" Fi was doubtful.

Agatha shook her head. "I'm not risking you dropping my prize-winning pumpkin! I'll ask them to unpin the side of the tent."

"Have you seen the Magewell entries this year?" The wizard with the marrow asked as he unloaded his vegetable with a flick of his staff. "You might get second place, I s'pose."

Agatha stared. "They're not even here yet…"

"No, but I went to the allotments last week. I tell you; anyone would think they'd used growing spells." He bustled past, levitating his marrow ahead of him. "Mind you, I bet they can't compete with my parsnip – want a sneak peek at the most humorous vegetable in the show?"

Without waiting for an answer, he pulled a vegetable from his pocket and showed it to the two sisters. The sisters schooled their faces into mirrors of carefully blank expressions.

"That's certainly an…unusual shape, Harris."

"Very, um, anatomical."

The wizard grinned and tucked his parsnip away.

Once they'd recovered from the shocking root vegetable, Agatha tapped her foot and bit her lip nervously. Fi patted her on the arm. "I'm sure he's just winding you up because he knows his marrow can't compete with your pumpkin."

Agatha nodded distractedly, then turned back to her truck. "I don't like using magic on it but if they don't have a crane…" She waved her hand, and the pumpkin wobbled into the air. It floated ahead of the nature witch as she made her way into the marquee. Her mother was inside with the clipboard. Fi wondered how she had got here so fast when she had been arguing with the coachload of witches in the next field.

"Agatha, good, glad you could make it. If you can put it down here, I think that will be best." Nell motioned distractedly to a pile of hay on the ground before spinning on her heel. "No, no Harris, I said the marrows were going over on this side of the tent. That table is for the fruit!" She bustled over to supervise the wizard and see his marrow was escorted to its proper place.

Agatha winced as she directed the pumpkin down a little too fast. It bumped onto the ground. Taking a cloth from her back pocket, she began rubbing the orange skin to a shine. Fi raised an eyebrow.

"Fi! Fi! What are you doing here? You should be in the refreshments tent." Nell waved a pen at her.

Fi took the hint and left. She retrieved the tins from her sister's truck but gave up trying to balance all of them. She'd have to make two trips. Walking carefully over the uneven grass, she craned her neck to find the refreshments tent. The site was a hive of activity, and she took a moment to watch the witches move from one area to another with focus. There was a marked increase in speed whenever someone caught Nell's eye.

Fi spotted a middle-aged witch with a coffee and headed in that direction. She soon found the large marquee with the hand-painted sign outside declaring prices for teas, coffees and juice. She moved past the short queue of people and joined Steve behind the trestle table where he was organising cakes into a display.

"I can't believe I let your mother bully me into running this stall!" he complained.

"You're too good natured to say no."

"That may be true, but it doesn't mean she didn't bully me!"

"You and half the village."

Steve grinned. "Are those your famous scones?"

"Hardly famous, but yes. You're not the only one Mum bullied. Where do you want them?"

Steve gestured to a large plate, and Fi started unpacking her tins. She piled the scones up erratically before shoving the empty tins under the table where they'd be out of sight behind the crisp white tablecloth.

"What's your secret?" Steve asked as he helped to stack the scones on the plate.

"Must be the magic sugar," Fi joked, although it was partly true. She used pixie branded sugar in all her baking.

"Hallo there! Is this where we can donate refreshments? I heard you were in need of some quality baked goods."

Fi looked up into the haughty face of Goody Winships. She recognised her mother's rival from previous WWWI events. The older witch was dogged by a similar aged witch with a round face, a snagged cardigan and a put-upon expression. Fi offered the smaller witch a sympathetic smile as Goody held her hand out expectantly, and her friend handed her a large sponge cake. Goody placed the cake at the front of the table with a flourish, pausing to admire the neat strawberry decoration around the edges.

"Thanks," Steve flashed her a smile and moved it to the back of the table next to the other sponges.

"I rather think it would look better here," Goody insisted as she reached for the plate and moved it back to the central position. The witch curled her lip as she appraised the rest of the selections on the cake table. Steve's eyes flashed and his teeth lengthened. Fi laid a comforting hand on his arm and felt him relax. Goody pursed her lips and raised an eyebrow before she turned and exited the tent. Her friend hesitated a minute and offered an apologetic smile before turning to follow. As she twisted around, her large bag swung over the table, and she knocked several scones to the floor.

"Sorry!" she bent over to retrieve the baked goods.

"That's a nice floral perfume," Steve commented, trying to put her at ease as he took the scones from her.

The smaller witch gave him a quick smile before she looked away, not seeming comfortable making eye contact. "It's just my flowers, from the garden." She scurried out of the tent to catch up with Goody Winships.

Once they were gone, Fi deliberately moved the large strawberry sponge to the back of the table. She shared a conspiratorial smile with Steve before heading to get the last of the scones from the truck.

Chapter 8

As Fi walked back from the truck with the remaining tins, she caught sight of her mother in conversation with her rival. Her eyes caught on the golden dragon-like creature sat regally at Goody's feet. The small wyrm almost glowed in the morning light. Goody had a smug smile on her face as she waved a piece of parchment in front of Nell's face. Nell herself sported a strained smile, but her eyes looked furious. Fi watched as her mother made her excuses and left, her face looking like she'd swallowed a wasp. With a shake of her head, Fi finished her trip to the refreshments tent, arriving at the same time as her mother.

"What was all that about?"

"What?" Nell snapped. "Oh, nothing…just Goody Winships winning a lifetime achievement award, that's all." Bitterness seeped into her voice. Nell took a breath and closed her eyes to compose herself. When she reopened them, her blue eyes blazed with anger. She shook the papers in her hand. "Have you seen these leaflets?"

Fi tried to focus on the offending papers as her mum waved them in front of her nose. "What's wrong with them? They look very professional and the pumpkin is nice and bright…"

"Halloween Hullabaloo! I bet Agatha put Liv up to this! She knew I didn't like the Samhain Spooktacular posters."

Fi covered her mouth to hide her grin at her sister's minor rebellion against their mother.

"How can I look the other chairs in the eye when this is what we're calling it?!" Her mother's eyes roamed the cake stall even as she ranted. "And really Fi, you could have stacked your scones more neatly, it looks like you just dumped them on the plate willy nilly!"

Fi looked at the offending pile of scones. "They're rustic…"

Her mother's arched eyebrow showed what she thought of that remark. Nell turned and noticed a warlock stacking teacups haphazardly. She shouted at the unsuspecting warlock and he sent the stack crashing to the ground. With a sigh, Nell bustled over to demonstrate exactly how to stack the teacups. Fi shook her head and decided to ignore her mum's veiled direction to restack the scones. Instead, she grabbed a cup of coffee from the refreshments stand and hurried outside before her mother could catch her. Outside, she found Agatha, sipping her own cup of coffee. Her sister looked furious.

"What's the matter?"

Agatha speared Fi with a look, her lips a thin line of anger. "It's not right!"

"What isn't?"

"Her!"

Fi's brows furrowed in confusion. "Mum?" she guessed.

Agatha let out a snort of laughter. "No, for once it's not Mum. It's that bloody Winships. She thinks she's so clever, well we'll see."

"What about her?"

"She brought in a pumpkin!"

Fi waited until it was clear that her sister wasn't going to say more. "And?"

"And it's bigger than mine! She thinks she's fooled everyone, well not this year! She's going to get what's coming to her."

Fi dodged her sister's waving finger and was about to ask what she meant when Effie bumped into her. The nonagenarian wore a beaded dress, but her usual neat hair was in a wild white frizzy halo around her head. She plucked at the sleeve of her coat and looked around in jerky movements.

"Morning Effie," Agatha acknowledged the older witch politely as she moved closer.

Effie nodded distractedly. "The bees…have you seen the bees today?"

"What about the bees?" Fi looked around, expecting to see a swarm flying towards them.

"The bees are angry!" Effie's eyes were wild, darting back and forth. She focused on Fi and gripped her arms surprisingly hard, considering she was so small. "The bees are angry," she repeated seriously. "I would have thought you'd be able to sense them with your powers…"

"My powers?" Fi was confused. What did electricity have to do with bees?

"They have a positive charge, don't they? Oh my, I haven't seen them this upset since the Beast of Bodmin destroyed their hive. I've got to warn her."

"Who?" asked Fi, but Effie wasn't listening. She shook her head and let go of Fi's arms before tottering towards the stage.

Fi watched her go before rubbing her arms to take away the sting of Effie's grasp. "What was all that about?"

Agatha shrugged. She might have replied except that the speaker system let off a whine before Nell's clipped voice sounded across the field.

Chapter 9

"Is this thing on?" Nell tapped the microphone three times, sending loud, crunchy sounds through the speaker system. Fi and Agatha walked over to the open space in the middle of all the marquees set up to host the various competitions and stalls for the fete. Their mother stood in the middle of a makeshift stage holding a microphone and looked like she was holding court over the proceedings.

Behind her sat the heads of the WWWI branches of St Columba's and Magewell, next to a bright-eyed wizard in a stereotypical long robe and pointed hat. There was also a striking lady wearing all black with an oversized pair of corgis sat at her feet. One of the corgi's tongues lolled out of its mouth, its breath steaming in the autumn air. She looked vaguely amused as she beamed at everyone watching the stage. Agatha caught sight of Neville and Bea and waved them over. Fi gave her niece a hug and nodded hello to her brother-in-law.

"Yes? Well, hello everyone and welcome to the annual Tri Village Halloween Fete. Thank you all for coming despite the change of location at such short notice and I must say it is a pleasure to see so many of our St Columba sisters and brothers here today and they are all looking so well." The St Columba contingent smiled awkwardly at the stage and looked embarrassed to be getting any attention. Fi could have sworn that some of them were a faint shade of green.

"My thanks also to our weather witches and wizards who have assured us of clear skies today." A gust of air buffeted the crowd, who laughed appreciatively.

"Yes, thank you. And of course, I have to mention the dedicated witches, wizards and werewolf at the refreshments stand. Cream teas and coffees will be available all day.

"Finally, I want to offer my thanks to all of you who have entered our competitions today. The competition tents are now sealed for judging. Joining me on the judging panel today are of course my fellow Witches', Wizards' and Warlocks' Institute chairs." Nell indicated Goody Winships and the portly St Columba Chairman, Greta Goosegog. Fi squinted; Greta was definitely the same colour as a limp lettuce. Goody stood and waved regally, her small wyrm preened itself by her side. "And today we are privileged to have both Nicholas the Mage and Madam Mim to open the Tri-Village Halloween Fete."

Nell stepped back from the microphone and clapped her hands together. A polite applause rippled around the field as

Nicholas and Madam Mim stepped forward. The corgis stayed put and took the opportunity to stretch out on the stage.

Nicholas waved and smiled down at the crowd. "Thank you for the warm welcome today. It is our privilege and honour to declare this Halloween Fete open and I, for one, am looking forward to judging the baking competition. I'm not making any predictions here, but I do love a good chocolate cake…"

It looked to Fi as if Madam Mim had just elbowed the senior member of the wizarding council in the ribs. He blinked up at her, his moustache working as if he was trying to figure out what to say. Madam Mim breezily leaned past him and spoke into the microphone, "Best of luck to all competitors and the fete is now open!"

Another round of applause spread across the field. Nell stepped forward and took the microphone again. "While we start the judging, which I guarantee will be fair and impartial," she shot a glare at Nicholas, "please enjoy the broomstick display from the Junior Witches' Brigade."

Nell clapped again before ushering her fellow judges off the stage towards the food tent to start the judging.

A troop of young witches dressed in black uniforms with yellow and black striped braid along the edges of their waist-length cloaks walked into the roped off circle that comprised the performing arena in front of the stage.

Agatha smiled and waved at members of her class who were taking part. Fi heard her niece whine about wanting to take part before being scooped up onto her father's shoulders.

A tall witch dressed in a midnight blue robe stood on the stage, nodding encouragingly. One of the young performers burst into tears at the pressure of performing and ran off to her parents, her long pigtails flying behind her.

The supervising witch on the main stage fiddled with a small music player, and strains of classical music filled the air. The tune was upbeat and fast. Fi racked her brains trying to place the familiar melody. The remaining children mounted their broomsticks carefully and set off. They completed a wobbly circle around the arena to cheers that must have come from doting parents and friends. Sita Kumar waved to her daughter as she took a stream of pictures on her smart phone.

After their first loop, the girls split into two smaller groups and travelled in opposite directions around the arena at carefully spaced distances from each other. The girls sped up until their outlines blurred into flashes of yellow and black zipping around the arena. Fi smiled as she finally placed the music: Flight of the Bumblebee.

Each group headed for the top of the circle before curving round and crossing each other's path with perfect precision. Fi thought she saw the supervising witch let out a relieved breath as the junior witches executed the manoeuvre. After they repeated the criss-cross figure of eight two more times, the witches pointed their broomsticks upwards and headed skywards. High above the arena, the witches circled again before dive-bombing towards the floor. Fi held her breath. Each of the witches pulled out of the dive before hitting the grassy ground. With triumphant smiles on their faces, the witches resumed their circling.

It was quite unfortunate that, on the easiest part of the routine, just before the end, one of the young girls urged their broomstick forward slightly too fast and nudged the bristles at the end of the girl in front's broom. The second girl spun out of control and careened into another girl, who fought to get control of her own broom and instead hit a fourth child. Soon there was a pile of crying children slumped in the arena with only one airborne girl who had avoided the crash zooming around the arena.

The witch on the stage ran down to attend to her charges as the music wound to an end. The single witch still in flight gracefully brought her broomstick to a halt, dismounted, and did a curtsy. The others got to their feet one by one and performed the most miserable set of curtsies Fi had ever seen. Many of them had tears running down their small faces.

The speaker system automatically played the next track, and the witch must have had her playlist on shuffle, as Fi was sure she did not mean for everyone in attendance to hear the beginnings of a rap about large butts. Mortified, the witch left the girls, who were now mostly being led away by parents with reassurances that they'd done very well and yes, they could have an ice cream.

Fi turned and frowned as she noticed that the resident ice cream man, who clearly knew a good thing when he saw it, was in the process of upping the price of his 99 cones with flakes by scrawling on the side of his pink truck with a thick marker pen.

The witch in blue finally managed to disconnect her device from the speaker system and Liv stepped up in an immaculate lavender suit to take over.

"I think we can all agree that the Junior Witches' Brigade did a lovely job and certainly provided a memorable opening display for our fete this year. Let's hear it for the girls!" An overenthusiastic applause with cheers sounded from everyone who had watched the display, overcompensating from the awkwardness and the morbid fixation with the crash. Liv waited for the applause to die down before carrying on her next announcement.

She stared at a white index card she was holding in her French manicured hand. "Firstly, I want to remind everybody that the lost and found is in at the refreshments tent. Steve has told me they've already had a watch and a phone handed in so if you're missing anything, head over there and grab a slice of cake while you're at it. They are simply divine, and all profits today are going to be split equally between the three WWWI branches and a local animal shelter.

"Now, while the judges are away deciding who's going to win Best in Show, I have been asked to welcome the animal agility teams from the three villages. Please give them all a big round of applause." Liv clapped again before stepping down from the stage.

She caught Fi's eye and headed over.

"Enjoying your day?"

"I'm not sure enjoy is the word…" Liv covered a yawn with her elegant hand.

"Tired?"

"You know the irony of the sleep therapist; we never get enough sleep ourselves. And last night I had the weirdest dream that something was going to go wrong…" Liv stared into the middle distance for a minute before shaking her head. "It was probably that crash. Poor things, broomstick riding is harder than it looks."

Fi nodded, remembering her own youthful attempts at mounting and controlling her own broomstick. She'd never seemed to get on with it and, much to her mother's chagrin, had been much more adept with a vacuum cleaner.

"How did Mum get you up on stage?"

"I felt I owed her after the second set of posters…and it was either agree to announcements or volunteer in the refreshments tent!"

Fi let out a curse word. Liv arched one perfect eyebrow at her as Fi sprinted off towards the refreshments tent. "Got to go, I'm meant to be on shift now!"

Liv's laughter sounded across the field behind her, making several male heads turn in the therapist's direction.

Chapter 10

Nell Blair's voice rolled across the field, amplified by the sound system. Fi sighed and stretched. The refreshments tent had been busy all morning, and both she and Steve, the other volunteer, had been run off their feet. But the temptation of the raffle was such that the stall was empty for the first time that day. Honestly, how much tea and cake did people need? Fi thought as she idly munched her way through one of the remaining biscuits that was less perfect than the others.

Glen, Steve's partner, had found them some chairs when he and Zadie had visited the tent to whisk Steve away to watch the magic animal display. Fi relaxed on hers as her mother's voice called out the winners. She angled herself so she could see the crowds. Agatha was on the balls of her feet in anticipation, while Neville stroked her hand, trying to soothe her nerves. Steve stood with his family in a similar pose while Glen tried to calm him.

Fi hadn't entered any of the competitions, but she had bought a set of tickets for the raffle. The prizes included an hour's sleep therapy with Liv as well as a crystal ball reading by Effie. She rolled her eyes. Personally, she had entered for the chance at winning the hamper of Cotswolds' produce provided by the local deli or the month's supply of hot chocolates.

Her phone buzzed. It was a message from Maxi, a Magical Liaison Office agent she'd met in Avalon when her mother had volunteered to help save the fae realm from attack by Mordred. He'd actually been fascinated by her power, instead of horrified, and she enjoyed his messages.

Hope you're having a shockingly good Halloween! X

She replied quickly and then tuned back to her mother's voice.

"Thank you, thank you. It is time for the hotly anticipated announcements of today's competition winners. Firstly, I would like to say that the standard of entries this year has impressed all of the judges. There was some debate around allowing judges themselves to enter the competitions," Nell turned pointedly to Goody Winships, "however, we have decided to allow it as the entries are anonymous until after the judging and this is, after all, a friendly competition." Nell's voice ground out the last words. "And now I will hand over to our guests of honour to announce the winners."

Nicholas the mage coughed. "I am delighted to say that the winner of the baking competition is Goody Winships with her lemon curd sponge." There was a smattering of applause as Goody Winships accepted her prize graciously with a sly smile.

"And we have a special runner's up prize for Steve Loupin who was a very close second with his delicious chocolate delight cake, although not everyone appreciated the hint of chilli. But, may I say, that it was one of the best cakes I have tasted, and I will be certain to get the recipe from him."

There was a smattering of applause as Steve loped onto the stage to collect his blue ribbon. His smile was tight as he shook the mage's hand.

"And we have a special mention for the under twelves bakers which goes to Angelica McLeaf for her fairy cakes made with real fairy dust."

More applause as a serious looking small girl with a jet-black plait stumbled up the steps onto the stage. She took her rosette carefully and then turned and marched back down the steps without waiting to shake the mage's hand. Steve grinned as he followed her off the stage. Madam Mim hid a laugh behind her hand as she took the microphone.

"Thank you, Nicholas, and I have the honour of announcing the winner of the largest vegetable competition. This year was hotly contested, and I am simply amazed how large some of these plants can get to. After careful measuring and weighing by our judges, the prize goes to Goody Winships with her humongous pumpkin with a special mention to Agatha Blair for her pumpkin, which missed out on the top prize by two centimetres."

Madam Mim put her hands together elegantly before pinning a ribbon to Goody Winships. Agatha stood to one side with her face like thunder. Fi glanced at the sky and was unsurprised to see purple clouds gather overhead, thick with rain and the promise of a coming storm.

"I am also told that it is customary to present a prize for the most humorous vegetable and the award this year goes to Harris Pages with his amusing parsnip. I won't say what it resembles as there are children present, but I will say that all the vegetables will remain on display for the remainder of the fete."

Nicholas stepped forward again, "And our next prize is for best animal in show. I'm told that for the past decade a golden wyrm belonging to Goody Winships has won the prize" Goody Winships started to stand, "…and while she is lovely, this year's best in show is an owlbear named Fluffy who belongs to Sita Kumar. I must say that this is the first time I have seen an owlbear in person and I am glad that Sita has tamed this one."

Goody sat down abruptly; her own pet curled at her feet hissed softly as Sita led the champion owlbear onto the stage to accept the rosette. The corgis stood and moved protectively in front of their mistress. Fi rubbed her eyes, certain that the beasts had morphed into something larger and more ferocious for a moment.

The owlbear ignored the hostile animals on the podium and shuffled forward. The seven-foot creature – a strange furry and feathered cross between a bear and a nightmare owl - and its petite owner made quite the contrast. The owlbear let out an ear-piercing shriek that was almost as bad as when Nell got too close to the speakers with the microphone as Sita took a quick selfie with the judges. It pecked at Nicholas' pointed hat with its sharp beak before Sita led it offstage. It turned its head a full one eighty degrees as it left, its golden eyes fixed on the star spotted hat, making a strange clicking noise with its pointed tongue.

The litany of prize winners continued as Nicholas and Madam Mim announced results for best pie, best jam, and the two drinks categories (alcoholic and non-alcoholic). Next up were the craft categories. These seemed endless to Fi: best crochet item, best knitted item, wool craft, something new from something old, embroidery…the list went on.

Goody Winships snagged a couple more blue ribbons and Fi could see some members of the audience grumble as she accepted them. Finally, they were onto the raffle.

Nell stepped forward, "Now we'll read out the winners one by one and if you can come up to the stage, I'll pass you your prizes. Madam Mim and Nicholas have decided to make this year's draw extra special, so I hand over to them."

Fi pulled her own set of raffle tickets from her pocket. She glanced down at the printed numbers on cheap coloured tickets. She squinted, unsure if the dull colour was meant to be green or blue. Three hundred to three hundred and five. Come on lucky numbers. There was a month's supply of hot chocolates from Effie's café on offer.

Madam Mim smiled enigmatically while Nicholas twirled his moustache before raising his staff into the air. He brought it down on the stage with a mighty crash and sparking blue smoke filled the stage. The smoke billowed away into the sky and formed a dragon. The smoky dragon swooped over the fete before melting into the sky. Everyone clapped at the illusion and turned back to the stage, where a large top hat now sat.

"A little cliché," murmured Madam Mim before she waggled her fingers over the silk hat. A small white bunny rabbit hopped out and into her outstretched hand. It handed her a small raffle ticket before leaping back into the hat. She smoothed out the number and leaned to the microphone, "Red ticket number one hundred and twelve."

That was the hamper gone, Fi huffed out a sigh of disappointment, but there was still the month of free hot chocolates.

Not to be outdone, Nicholas created a miniature whirlwind to carry up the next ticket. He allowed it to swirl into the sky before he reached out and grabbed it with his aged hand. He read out the number. Fi watched a small boy jump off the ground with excitement before his father accompanied him to the side of the stage to collect his prize from Nell.

The mage and sorcerer competed for the most elaborate raffle ticket draw good naturedly, drawing many oohs and aahs from the spectators. Fi crushed her tickets in her palm as the hot chocolates went to a green-skinned wizard from St Columba's. She let out a curse word under her breath and decided to focus on watching the excellent display of magic.

Fi thought Madam Mim clinched the best magic of the raffle with a flock of birds that soared above the field until one came to land in her hand and transformed into a ticket. Fi enjoyed the trick so much that she missed her number.

"Green number three hundred and three… are you there three hundred and three?"

"Me! That's me!" Fi shrieked, dropping her tickets in her excitement. She scrabbled around on the floor for them and rushed forward. She practically ran to the side of the stage where her mum handed her a bottle of wine. It wasn't the hamper or the month of free hot chocolates, but it was something.

It must have been the last prize as well because she heard Madam Mim say something about it being a pleasure to be here as she rested one long hand on the head of the tan and black corgi. Fi stood awkwardly on stage, gripping the bottle as the sorceress continued.

"And now our judges will do a short flyby on broomsticks before we take a fifteen-minute break before the main event – the best trick competition. All comers are welcome, and I believe there is a sign-up sheet outside of the craft tent for any last-minute competitors."

Fi was vaguely aware of the buzz behind her as the judges descended the stage. A shout broke through the sound of people making their way to the temporary toilet facilities.

Chapter 11

Fi turned, trying to see over the press of the crowd as she followed Madam Mim down the steps.

"What are you saying?" Goody Winships voice sounded annoyed, pressing her hands to her temples. Her breath came rapidly.

"I'm saying that it's over!" Fi recognised her sister's earthy tones. She sighed and hurried down the steps to try to calm things down. "Your reign of deceit is over! You're not going to get away with it anymore!"

"Wha- wha- wha-" Goody Winships gagged, panting now.

"That's right! You haven't got anything to say, have you? It's over."

"Agatha!" Fi put a hand on her sister's arm.

Agatha spun round. "What?! It's about time someone called her out!"

Freed from the incensed witch, Goody raised her hand shakily and summoned her broomstick. It flew towards her, nudging Agatha to one side as it settled in a horizontal position at the perfect height for Goody to sit on. She took up a side-saddle position, her chest heaving as she panted. Beads of sweat formed on her forehead.

"Are you alright?" Fi asked. Was Goody normally that pale?

The small golden wyrm sitting regally at the front of the broomstick turned to look at its owner and tilted its head to one side. With a disdainful look at the two sisters, Goody didn't reply. Instead, she kicked off and joined the other judges in the air.

"What did you do that for? She was about to confess to cheating!" Agatha stormed off.

Fi let her go and headed in the opposite direction, back towards the food tent. Halfway back, she paused and turned to watch the flying display. There was a bit of an argy bargy as Nell and Goody both jostled for first position, but in the end, they allowed Madam Mim to lead the flight with as much graciousness as either of them could muster.

Nicholas ignored the broomsticks and instead made use of a staff, which he rode like a surfboard, his long robe flapping behind him as he ascended into the air. Members of the public directly below his billowing robes hastily looked away as he passed overhead, and they got a clear answer to the perennial question of whether a wizard wore anything under his robes.

Both WWWI Chairs sat with ramrod straight backs as they circled the field. During the second circuit, Goody sagged and fell behind. Beads of sweat broke out on her face as she urged her broomstick to keep up with the others. The golden wyrm perched at the front of the handle looked back at her mistress. Nell allowed herself a small smile. Goody's broomstick skills had suffered in the past year. With a small, regal wave to the crowd, the judges acknowledged the smattering of applause before they started their descent.

Abruptly, Goody's broomstick turned into a nosedive straight for the spectators. Fi gaped at the risky trick, performed at a much higher speed than the junior witches' display earlier in the morning. The crowd 'oohed' and 'aahed' as they watched her dangerous descent. Nell shook her head and muttered under her breath; something about the witch being a show-off.

The broomstick juddered and bucked under Goody's hands. The crowd's appreciation turned to horror as the witch angled lower and lower. People darted left and right to try to clear the way. A young boy stood stock still in front of Fi, wailing for his Mum.

Fi watched as Goody's broomstick seemed to aim straight for the child. Tears streamed down his face as he screamed. The small wyrm jumped free with a shriek, its golden wings opening fully as it glided to safety. Fi ran forward. She knocked the boy to one side as Goody lifted her arms from the handle and held them over her face. Fi twisted, but it was too late. The witch crashed into her.

Chapter 12

Fi blinked awake. Her senses came back to her in waves. First, the pain; her head throbbed, and her body felt like someone had driven over her. Dimly, she realised that she was on the ground, a heavy weight pressed on her stomach. Her neck was twisted to one side and her head pressed against the cool, damp ground. Sound came next; panicked screams. Finally, her sight came into focus.; she studied a large splinter of wood that lay between fat, green blades of grass. A ladybird climbed over it. The bug looked at Fi and spoke her name. Fi frowned. Since when did ladybird's talk? And how could it even talk if it wasn't moving its lips? And how did it know her name?

She turned her head away from the insect and realised two things. Firstly, it was her sister shouting her name as she kneeled next to Fi and secondly that there was another face much closer to her own. So close that a beaked nose almost touched her cheek. Fi blinked and Goody Winships' frozen features came into focus.

Fi tried to scream.

Agatha rolled the older lady's body off of her sister and Fi felt the weight lift from her chest.

"Are you OK? Where are you hurt?"

Fi groaned and attempted to sit up. She waved her sister away, before she realised her sister wasn't talking to her. She turned to look at Goody. The witch's arm was bent at an unnatural angle. Agatha moved around to the prone witch and loosened the silk scarf around the elder lady's throat.

"Give her space!" a reedy voice protested, bending down and pushing Agatha back. Fi recognised Goody's friend from the refreshments tent and gently pulled her sister away from the collapsed woman.

"Doctor – get a doctor!" Agatha stammered. She backed away another step before turning and shouting, "A doctor! Is anyone a doctor?!"

The gaggle of people who had gathered around Goody's prone form looked between one another and shrank back.

"I'm a doctor," a low voice sounded.

"Here, over here!" Agatha shouted, panic mounting in her voice.

Fi lay back down; it was much comfier on the grass than trying to sit up. She watched in a detached sort of way as a man crouched over Goody Winships. She tried to make sense of what had happened. Goody had crashed. Into her. She nodded. Her eyes found the shard of broomstick in the grass again. The broomstick had shattered on impact. Impulsively, she reached for it, murmuring an apology to the ladybird as she did so. She put it in her pocket, feeling that it was important somehow.

The man, presumably a doctor, looked up. He met Fi's eyes and shook his head.

Someone screamed. A member of the St John's ambulance team pushed through. He had expected to be dealing with the odd sprained ankle or person who'd drank too much; now he put the old witch onto her back and started resuscitation.

"How can she be gone so suddenly?" another watcher murmured.

Fi felt like she was in a daze. A flash brought her back to the present. She turned to glare at a photographer from the local paper.

"Stop that!" Fi was furious. No one had liked Goody, but surely she deserved some respect in death. She pushed herself up onto an elbow. Her power flared. Fi fought to get it under control, but it was too late. She felt it spiralling through her body in sparking waves. She desperately sought a means to focus the surge before she destroyed everyone's phone. Her hair stood on end with the static charge.

She pointed a finger at the digital camera in the journalist's hand and let loose. The camera let out a small, underwhelming hiss. The journalist let out an undignified squeal at the sudden electric shock and dropped the camera to the floor. All that power and you'd think there'd be more to show. Behind the photographer, Sita delicately put her own camera phone back in her pocket.

Her own phone heated in her back pocket. Fi swore. She'd managed to short out her own smartphone as well as the camera. At least she had her trusty Nokia brick phone at home to tide her over until she got a new mobile. That thing was indestructible and impervious to her power surges.

The crowd backed away now as a couple of marshals in high-vis vests took control of the situation.

The doctor turned to Fi. "Are you alright?"

She looked into his deep, brown eyes and lost her words. She felt her cheeks flush.

"Let me take your pulse." He filled the awkward silence as Fi stared, having apparently completely lost her power of speech.

He reached for her wrist.

"Ouch!"

Fi jerked back and then tried not to react, even though she had felt the spark of her power flow from the point where his fingers had touched her skin.

"Are you alright?" she asked timidly, echoing his words.

He smiled back at her. "Yeah, just surprised, that's all. That was some strong static electricity."

Fi latched onto the rational explanation. "Yes, yes, weird. Ha ha ha." Better he think that it was static than know that she couldn't control her powers when her emotions were high. And she didn't want to think about what was behind those feelings as she met his dark eyes again.

He looked into her eyes and frowned, "You might have concussion." He pulled out a small torch attached to a keychain and shone it into her eyes. She flinched under the intense light and tried to pull away. She turned her head and was immediately accosted by a wet tongue.

"Urgh!" she threw up her hands to shield herself from the attack of licks from a large, slobbery dog. Unperturbed, the dog transferred its hot tongue to her hands.

"Rus! Stop that! Sorry, he gets excited. I mustn't have tied him up properly when I ran over."

"He's your dog?" Fi tore her eyes away from the huge black mastiff to the doctor.

He nodded and finally pulled the dog away from Fi. "Sit!" he ordered. The dog sat and licked its jowls, looking very pleased with itself. He turned his attention back to his patient. After checking her over, the doctor declared that she hadn't broken anything.

"Thanks Dr…"

"Everyone calls me Mort."

"Right, well thanks Dr Mort. I'm Fi by the way, well Fiona but everyone calls me Fi." She realised she was babbling and stopped talking abruptly.

There was a moment of awkward silence.

Agatha strode over, putting her phone away. "The police are here."

Chapter 13

Dr Mort stood and offered Fi his hand. Fi clamped her powers down and allowed herself to be pulled upright. She moaned a little as she got up, her aching body protesting at the movement.

A mousy woman stood nearby, her eyes on the body. Fi recognised her as the witch who had been with Goody at the refreshments stall. Goody's friend fidgeted with her bag, her eyes on the medics as they worked to resuscitate the witch.

"She was a friend of yours, wasn't she?"

The woman jumped, but quickly regained her composure. "Yes, we were very close. And now…" she dissolved into tears.

Fi looked around helplessly. She was no good at dealing with emotions. Luckily, the doctor took charge, "Why don't you come with us? You might be in shock."

He led them both to the small St John's ambulance tent and sat them down in folding wooden chairs. Another medic handed them both a space blanket to ward off any cold before offering them sweet tea from a heated urn in the tent. He handed Fi two paracetamol from a first aid kit.

Fi took the tablets gratefully and washed them down with the tea, wishing it were coffee.

"She's dead…"

Fi stopped herself from turning to look at the volunteers gossiping behind her and took another sip of her drink. She grimaced. Why didn't they have coffee? Why was she so unlucky?

A young man in a police officer's uniform stepped inside the tent and interrupted her introspection. For a second, Fi thought he was a teenager playing dress up before she realised that the uniform was genuine. He looked from the two seated women to the tall doctor.

"I was told there were some witnesses in here?"

"I'm the doctor who…examined her, before they started CPR."

The police officer nodded along. "They're still going but it's pretty obvious she's…gone. They'll confirm it at the hospital. The ambulance is on its way, just navigating the country lanes and some badly parked coaches. I'll take a statement from you in a minute. And who are you then?" He turned his gaze to Fi.

"Fiona Blair. I, uh, was hit by Goody. I mean, she crashed into me when she, uh, crashed."

"Ri-ight. I'll need to take a statement from you, too. And you?"

Goody's friend stared blankly at the canvas tent.

"Madam?"

She jerked her head round to look at the officer. Fi thought she looked very small and alone. "I'm Margaret, Goody's…her friend. It's just, I mean, it's all so sudden, I can't…it's so strange."

The young officer nodded along in what he thought was a sympathetic manner, "OK, I'll get a statement from you as well." He whipped out a pristine pad of paper and a biro. "Who's first?"

Margaret put up her hand meekly and shuddered. "I want to get it over with. I just want to get home. She should never have tried that stupid trick…"

Fi frowned, "So, she was planning to try a nosedive?"

"Well, I mean, she didn't say anything to me about it, but she always liked to be the centre of attention…."

While Margaret answered the officer's questions, Fi thought about the dive. It was a risky trick for any witch or wizard to pull off but for an elderly lady on what was supposed to be a gentle fly around the ring for the judges…something didn't feel right. Even if she had wanted to show off, surely Goody would have pulled up rather than crash.

And the broomstick had been shaking, she was sure of it. Had someone bespelled the broom to deliberately cause Goody to crash? She shook her head. It was a crazy thought. She jolted out of her thoughts and realised that the policeman was staring at her.

"Sorry, can you repeat the question?"

"I said, can you tell me what happened?"

"Oh, right, yes. I was standing, watching the flight when she, Goody that is, started to look like she was out of control. She dived towards the crowd. There was a boy…I pushed him out of the way, and then, I got hit…I mean, Goody crashed into me. But, look, I think there was something wrong with the broom."

"Oh?" the young man arched one bushy eyebrow.

"It was acting odd. Maybe it was enchanted. Maybe someone wanted to kill her!"

His face scrunched up in disbelief before he switched back to a professionally neutral expression and wrote it down. "OK, well that's something we'll look into." He puffed out his chest. "You can be assured that we are getting statements from everyone who's here today and we will be exploring all avenues."

"But…"

"Yes?"

Fi opened her mouth, then shut it again. "Nothing," she muttered.

"Now, if I could speak to you outside, doctor?"

Fi kicked her feet on the floor in annoyance, getting grassy stains on her vintage Converse trainers. She had seen the look on the officer's face. They weren't going to look into her suspicions at all. She stuffed her hands inside her pockets and almost jumped as her fingers brushed against the piece of wood. She had a bit of the broomstick with her. Maybe she could do her own investigating. The idea tantalised her, much more interesting than a job search.

Agatha popped her head into the tent. "How are you?" Agatha's voice was laced with concern.

"Fine, I guess."

"Mum's waiting outside. Are you ready to go home or do you need more time?"

Fi stared at her feet.

"I was in the livestock tent earlier, thought they looked a bit *sheep*ish."

Fi's eyes snapped up to her sister. Agatha was trying to make her feel better with bad puns. It worked.

"Not *ram*bunctious then?"

"Hark at ewe!"

"Ewe're terrible!"

Agatha shook her head. A half smile curled up Fi's face as she debated staying with the St John's ambulance people and avoiding her mother, who'd probably find some way to blame Fi for the accident. Instead, Fi sighed and stood. "I'm ready."

Fi felt the faintest whisper of something tug at the edge of her mind.

She was killed.

"Did you hear something?" Fi looked around.

"No," Agatha cocked her head, "Nothing. Are you sure you're alright to come home?" She looked around for a medic.

Fi shook her head and pushed her way through the tent flap to the field. Now she was hearing voices. Great.

Chapter 14

Cressida, the wyrm formerly belonging to Goody Winships, shook her head. If it was possible for a wyrm to tut with annoyance, she would have done so. She had somehow connected psychically with someone in the crowd, but the witch was moving away. The small golden wyrm wriggled her way through the bystanders' legs, trying not to touch any of the mucky shoes. She hissed loudly when a boot trod on her tail, but kept moving. She couldn't lose the connection. She pushed her thoughts away from the crushing emptiness that had coursed through her when she realised she couldn't feel the familiar pull of Goody's mind.

The new psychic link was tenuous, the faintest sliver of a thread between her and a human. Well, a supernatural. She shuddered. She hoped it was a witch. She'd hate to be psychically linked to, say, a werewolf. The wyrm shook her head and refused to entertain that thought. No, it had to be a witch.

Except right now, the one witch she could communicate with was heading away and didn't even appear to have heard her. She moved forward, unwilling to let this chance at companionship pass.

It was unbearable, she thought, as she slunk past a large white marquee. Her keen sense of smell could pick up the scents of cakes and the bitter aromas of tea and coffee. Why people, magic and mundane, chose to drink the stuff, she could never understand. But then she wasn't exactly fussy. A plain bottle of sparkling mineral water, preferably French, would do her.

Cressida continued with her mission to find the witch, ignoring the pang of loneliness that coursed through her. She'd never again enjoy her favourite brand of water or, a succulent rare steak sat across the table from her friend. She sped up.

She was closer now. She darted across the muddy ground; the grass churned by the hundreds of muddy feet who had turned up to this fete. She crouched behind a haystack and tried to ignore the young couple balancing on it sucking each other's faces. Disgusting. She peeked round, her golden eyes narrowing.

There was a small coven of three witches standing next to a portly man in some sort of dark uniform. Policeman. The word crossed her mind. Good. He could help with Goody's death. Now she just had to identify the witch she could speak to. Her eyes scanned the three women. The eldest one she recognised as Goody's arch-rival, Nell Blair. The wyrm's eyes narrowed into slits. She hoped she wasn't linked to that witch. Although, she noted, taking in the demure tweed suit, single strand of pearls and neat silvery-white bun, at least the woman had style, which seemed to be more than could be said for the other two witches.

One of them had dirt on her hand and under her fingernails, for goodness' sake! And the tartan trousers not only did nothing for her squat figure, but clashed with the orangey red top. Her hair was slung into a scruffy bun at the base of her neck. No, it couldn't be her, surely?

Cressida's eyes turned to the final candidate. This one had blonde hair stuck out around her head like she'd been stuck into a socket. She wore a scruffy trench coat over leggings with some sort of flat trainer with stars on it. The wyrm's lip curled. She had some idea what Goody would say about that look. If she were still alive. Cressida gulped. Wyrms couldn't cry, of course; no tear ducts, but the realisation that her companion, who she had known since she was a hatchling at the dwarf's wyrm farm, was gone hit her suddenly.

She had to know who she had found who might be able to, not replace exactly, but become some sort of surrogate for the relationship she'd had with Goody. She sent out a psychic call.

Can you hear me?

The witch with the sticking out blonde hair turned to the haystack. Cressida had her human. Without pausing to give the offending trainers a moment's more thought, she raced

across the field and leapt, using her small wings to give her
lift.

Chapter 15

Fi screamed. A small blur of gold jumped into her arms. Her first instinct was to get the creature off of her, so she shook her arms. Claws bit into her skin. She screamed again. The policeman took a step back and pulled out his Taser, pointing it at Fi as he tried to get a shot. Agatha swatted at the reptile with her slouchy handbag. The wyrm hissed and struggled for purchase in Fi's arms. Nell stood with her mouth in a perfect circle.

"That's Goody's wyrm!"

The creature climbed onto Fi's shoulders. Fi swiped at it.

Stop it!

"You're hurting me."

If you stay still, I won't have to hurt you.

The voice sounded reasonable. Fi stopped trying to prise the wyrm off her body, panting as she regained her composure after the shock. Agatha raised her handbag again. The police officer stepped to one side and aimed his Taser at the small dragon-like animal. The wyrm sank its claws deeper into Fi's shoulder and hissed.

"Don't!" Fi shrieked desperately, turning to block her sister's attack, "Ouch! Will you stop it?! It's talking to me somehow."

It is a she, if you don't mind.

"She's talking to me."

Nell's eyes were now as wide as her mouth, "*You* have a familiar link with Goody Winships' familiar?!"

"No need to sound so surprised!" Fi reacted instinctively to her mother's shocked tone.

Agatha's expression turned from warrior determined to protect her sister to interested teacher. "A familiar link…interesting. What would you say it feels like?"

"Er…"

Like the most thrilling thing that has ever happened to you, I'd imagine.

"No! I mean, it's weird. It… ouch! I mean she is speaking in my head," Fi glared at the wyrm now curled around her shoulders. "I know that was on purpose."

Cressida looked as innocent as a creature can when it knows it has deliberately clawed the person talking to it.

"Can it understand you, too?"

"I don't know!" Fi turned back to the wyrm, "Can you?"

The wyrm rolled its eyes.

"I think that means yes."

"Ladies, if you don't mind." The three women snapped their attention back to the older police officer who was clearly more in charge than the younger one Fi had encountered in the medical tent. "I've got your contact number, Mrs Blair, so I think that's everything."

She was killed.

It took Fi a moment to realise what the wyrm was talking about. "What?"

"I said I'll be going now," the policeman repeated with a frown, thinking that Fi was talking to him.

No!

"No! I mean, er, do you think it was a natural death?"

The policeman squinted at the witch. "Well, it was very sudden and obviously dramatic…but she was elderly…"

"I beg your pardon! Good Winships was only a year older than me! And I assure you that I have no intention of dying any time soon."

Something in her tone must have alerted the police officer. "You didn't get on then I take it." He turned his squinting gaze to Nell.

"We respected each other as fellow Chairs of WWWI branches."

"Why would you say it wasn't a natural death, Miss?"

"Hmm? Oh well, like I told the other policeman, I thought I saw the broomstick jolting, and, er, the wyrm said she was killed."

The officer only blinked twice at that proclamation. "And how does the wyrm know?"

Everyone looked expectantly at the golden dragon-like creature. Nothing.

"How do you know?" Fi prompted.

The wyrm flicked its tail. *She smelled wrong.*

"She says that Goody smelled wrong…" Fi petered out. It sounded ridiculous.

"I see." Fi could sense that the policeman was trying to be polite. "Well in cases like this, it's usual to perform an autopsy to determine the exact cause of death of course, and as she was a witch, I expect the Magical Liaison Office will be involved, so maybe I should take your number as well, Miss?"

"Blair. Fiona Blair." Fi reeled off her number and the policeman diligently wrote it down. He turned to go again.

"Wait a minute! What am I meant to do with this?" Fi gestured to the wyrm around her neck.

"Well, I could arrange for a magical animal sanctuary to pick it up."

Nell looked shocked. "It's your familiar now! You have a duty to her."

"But, but…"

"I've got to be going, but I'll pass your details on if you don't mind looking after it until the sanctuary can arrange collection? Probably be during the week, I imagine, if they're not too busy. Good day, ladies." He turned and walked off quickly to talk to the doctor, who stood next to the ambulance that had been called.

The three women, and the golden wyrm, watched as the paramedics loaded Goody Winships into the back of the ambulance and shut the doors.

"Well, I didn't realise she'd go that far to avoid competing in the best trick competition!"

"Mum!"

"Of course, I didn't mean it, but she'll be laughing up at me from whichever circle of hell she's gone to knowing that she's ruined my fete!"

"Mum!"

"She always liked to have the last laugh." Nell took in the twin expressions of disbelief on her daughters' faces. "Well, she did." Nell sighed, "I suppose I'd better close the fete." The elder witch walked towards the stage with a straight back.

"I'd better go find Bea and Neville," Agatha scanned the crowd, "I think I saw them head for the bouncy castle. Come on."

Fi shook her head. "I'll see you at the car."

Agatha nodded and walked off in the direction of the Bounce a Lot castle.

Fi headed to the car park. "And what," she mused as she looked at the wyrm still perched smugly on her shoulders, "am I supposed to do with you?"

Chapter 16

"Don't even think about it!" Fi glared at the golden wyrm balancing on her windowsill.

Think about what? Cressida blinked her green eyes innocently before taking a step forward. She picked her way carefully between the owl figurines lining the wooden sill. Fi held her breath. She watched the animal traverse the thin ledge. Just as she reached the end, the wyrm gave a flick of her tail and a grey pottery owl hit the floor. It smashed.

Oops.

"You did that on purpose!" Fi lunged forward and wrestled a damp tea towel over the wyrm's head. She ignored the sound of the remaining figurines crashing on the hard slate floor.

Let me go!

Fi heard the sharp intake of breath that usually preceded fire from the wyrm's throat. She felt the heat as Cressida let her fire loose. The damp tea towel sizzled, and the printed bumblebee design smoked slightly, but it didn't burst into flame. Fi allowed herself a small smile. This was the first time that she was anywhere close to besting the cat-sized creature since they had got home yesterday, and it had only cost her almost all of her ornaments.

I was only doing you a favour. That grey owl was hideous.

"That grey owl was a present!"

From someone who didn't like you?

"From my ex!" Fi realised too late that she hadn't helped her case. She was unemployed and arguing with an animal. And losing. Surely this was a new low.

The doorbell rang, interrupting the silence that stretched between the wyrm twitching under the tea towel and the witch. Fi stood. The wyrm squirmed free and jumped up onto the kitchen counter. Fi scowled at the creature.

"Stay still and don't break anything else!"

Fi practically sprinted to the front door. She was glad of the interruption. The small wyrm had been relentless in finding new ways to torment her all last night and she was wary of the dragon-like creature that could speak in her mind.

The wyrm – Cressida, apparently – had looked down on everything in Fi's home and had taken it upon herself to improve the living quarters by destroying anything she didn't like. Which meant practically everything that Fi owned.

Who is it?

Fi ignored the voice in her head and welcomed Glen into her home with a hug, "Hi Glen, thanks for coming."

"Not at all. You said you had something for me to look at?"

Fi hopped from one foot to the other as another tinkling of crockery smashing on slate tiles sounded through the downstairs.

Glen cocked his head. "What was that? Is someone else here?"

Fi abandoned her guest and dashed back to the kitchen. She stifled the expletive that came to her mouth as she took in the mess. She rushed forward and rescued another ornament from the side as Cressida's tail whipped round, intending to knock it to the floor along with the others.

Glen's brow creased as he saw the small wyrm crouched on the kitchen side.

Fi sighed. "Glen, meet Cressida. She's…staying with me. For now."

Cressida hissed and ran out of the room. Her sharp claws skittered on the wooden floor and floorboards creaked as the creature headed upstairs.

"Sorry about that. She's temperamental." Fi sighed again and cleaned up the mess before offering her neighbour a hot drink. The werewolf accepted a cup of tea gratefully.

He placed his small leather doctor's bag down by the table, sank into the chair and took a sip of his tea. "Maybe she's feeling nervous or lonely."

Fi tapped her fingers against her thigh. Maybe the wyrm was lonely and nervous, but she was also a pain in the ass. She changed the subject. "Thanks for bringing your kit."

Glen nodded and his eyes twinkled with curiosity. "Of course, are you going to tell me why I brought it?"

"So, I, er, found this bit of wood and I think it might be magical, but I hoped you might be able to tell me for sure."

Glen raised an eyebrow. "Where is it then?"

Fi rummaged in a drawer and withdrew the large splinter of wood she had taken from the fete. She placed it carefully on the table and sat opposite the werewolf.

Glen bent down and studied the wood with his honey-coloured eyes. He sniffed it then bent down to open his brown, leather bag. He retrieved a pair of tweezers and picked up the wood, twisting it so he could examine the grain.

"It's magical alright, I can smell it."

"What sort of magic is it?" Fi leaned forward.

Glen raised an eyebrow again and pulled out a bottle of purple liquid from his bag. He put on a pair of thick-lensed glasses and then delicately used a pipette to extract a small amount of the oozing potion. He paused, holding the pipette over the wood. Fi leaned back, and squinted her eyes half closed in anticipation of an explosion.

Glen allowed a single drip to drop from the plastic pipette onto the wood. Fi closed her eyes and pushed her chair further back. Nothing happened. She opened them again. Glen focused on the wood, frowning as he twisted it back and forth. His lenses shone green in the morning light.

He placed the wood carefully back on the table and removed his glasses.

"This wood has been enchanted to fly, I'd say it was part of a broomstick," he licked his lips. "If I had to guess, I'd say it had one previous owner. A powerful witch. And it's recently been in a crash."

"Wow, you can tell all that from that tiny splinter? Are there any other enchantments on it?"

He shook his head. "That's it. What were you expecting?"

"Oh, uh, nothing, I guess."

Glen narrowed his eyes at the witch, and strange shadows appeared on his face, but his voice was calm. "You know I can tell when you're lying. Your heartbeat speeds up and you start sweating. Is there something else you want to tell me?"

Fi couldn't meet his eyes. Instead, she sipped her drink, allowing the strong bitter taste of the Goblin Blend coffee to coat her mouth. The werewolf waited.

"OK, well, you probably heard what happened the other day at the fete…"

Glen nodded. "Steve told me what happened, I had to leave early with Zadie. Such a shame. We've bought potions from her before."

"Yeah, well, just before the, uh, crash, I thought I saw the broomstick buck like someone had cursed it. So, I…"

"So, you took a piece and thought you'd get me to examine it instead of telling the police?"

"Sorry, I should have told you in the first place, but the police already think I'm crazy and hearing voices. I tried to explain it was the wyrm, but they don't believe me. They wouldn't listen to me, so I wanted to be sure…Sorry." Her shoulders slumped.

He sighed. "It's OK. The police already had me look at some of the broomstick shards."

"You already knew?!"

"What did you expect? I'm the only magical antique dealer in twenty miles; of course, they asked me."

"Why didn't you tell me?"

"Why didn't you just tell me what you were really up to?" He echoed back her words. "You know, you should leave this to the police, Fi, and focus on yourself. The crash must have been traumatic, and you've got a lot going on. Maybe you should process that instead of chasing a police investigation."

Fi stared out the window as they finished their drinks. Her mind ignored Glen's suggestion and pondered the events of the fete. So, if it wasn't the broomstick, then what killed Goody Winships?

Chapter 17

A couple of hours later, Fi was back at the door. She took in the medium-sized man with the balding head standing on her doorstep. "Hello, er…"

The police officer rummaged in his thick coat pocket and held up his badge. "Detective Inspector Ledd. May we come in?"

Fi peered around the officer and noticed the willowy frame of Madam Mim standing on the path behind him. This afternoon, the iconic witch wore an old-fashioned black lacy dress that made her seem as if she was floating along the garden path. Fi stepped back to let them in.

"Of course, please come in, straight through into the kitchen." She glanced around. The wyrm had made herself scarce since Glen's visit.

Fi shut the door behind Madam Mim and followed D.I. Ledd and Madam Mim into the kitchen. They stood politely to one side in the small space, allowing Fi to enter. She stifled the expletive that came to her mouth as she saw the golden lizard on her kitchen side. She rushed forward, but it was too late. Cressida's tail whipped round and knocked a ceramic mug to the floor. It smashed with a loud ringing sound.

"I'll just get this mess cleaned up then I'll be right with you," Fi said with clenched teeth before she lunged for the wyrm. Cressida looked pleased with herself and grinned down at the shards of pottery in a dragon-ish sort of way. She darted to the side, but Fi managed to grab the wyrm behind its neck and pin it to the countertop.

"That was my favourite mug!" Fi hissed.

Really? It was vile. Why don't you have any cups and saucers?

Fi felt her power rising alongside her frustration. She allowed a small amount to trickle through her hand onto the wyrm's thick hide. The animal wriggled like it was being tickled. Fi let out a huff of breath, lifted the animal off the counter and gripped it tightly. She looked around for somewhere to lock it up, but the only room with a lock was the bathroom and Fi didn't want the wyrm destroying her chic white suite.

"Trouble with your familiar?" Madam Mim asked with an enigmatic smile flickering around her lips.

"Not my familiar." Fi thought she saw the wyrm stick out its forked tongue. "The sooner the magical animal sanctuary can get here and take her away, the better."

Cressida narrowed her green eyes and sank her teeth into Fi's arm. Fi screamed and dropped the wyrm. The reptile ran upstairs. Fi heard the patter of scaly feet as Cressida ran across the wooden hallway. Fi considered going after the wyrm but decided against it. Instead, she rubbed at her arm. The creature hadn't broken the skin at least. Maybe she'd overreacted by screaming. She dug around in a cupboard to hide her red face, found a brush and dustpan and began sweeping.

"Can I offer you a cup of tea or something?" Fi remembered her manners after she'd consigned the shards of pottery to the bin.

"Yes please, tea if you have it." Madam Mim accepted the offer graciously and Fi put the kettle on. She was desperately curious to know why they were here, but the noisy sound of boiling water prohibited conversation. So, she busied herself with finding mugs that hadn't been broken and offering milk and sugar. Once the kettle had boiled, she handed the mugs out, realising that she'd accidentally made the detective's in one shaped like a pig. He took it without comment and thanked her.

"Shall we sit, Ms Blair?"

"Oh, right, yes, please sit down," Fi indicated the wooden chairs around a tiny circular table that was her attempt to create a kitchen diner in a space far too small. The detective's chair scraped the wall as he settled into his seat.

"What can I do for you, Detective Inspector?"

"You were at the Halloween Fete?"

"Yes, of course. The entire village was there. Well three villages, actually. It's the Tri-Village Fete so there's three…"

Fi forced herself to take a sip of her sweetened coffee to stop her babbling. Madam Mim smiled at her kindly.

"And you were manning the refreshments stand?"

"Yes, for part of the day and I helped with set up."

"And who provided the refreshments?" Fi stared at him blankly. "I mean, who made them?"

"Oh, well, I made the scones and Steve made a cake. I think Goody Winships brought a sponge cake by and Effie did the sandwiches, she runs the café."

"I see." D.I. Ledd made a note in a pocketbook with a pen. "And did you serve Goody Winships yesterday?"

Fi thought. "No, I don't think so. She was in the tent to drop off her cake and then I didn't see her in the marquee the rest of the day. Maybe she came in when I had a break. Steve was on the stall most of the day, except when he went out to watch the animal show, and when he went up on stage."

"Yes, he won the…" D.I. Ledd consulted his notebook, "…baking competition?"

Fi nodded automatically then shook her head. "No, he came runner up. Goody Winships was the winner."

"She won a few awards yesterday, then?"

"Yes, I think it upset a few people."

"I see," he made another note.

Fi frowned, "What's this about?"

"Am I right in thinking that you told my colleague that Goody Winships was killed?"

"Yes, yes, I did. Are you looking into it?"

"And how did you come by that information?" He ignored her question.

"The wyrm told me," Fi was aware of how stupid it sounded, "And I thought I saw the broomstick...never mind."

"Why would you mention the broomstick?" the detective's eyes narrowed.

"Uh, well I noticed it was shaking when she was flying round, and I spoke to her friend, and she said Goody hadn't mentioned anything about doing that trick, so I thought it might have been cursed. And I, uh, found a piece and thought it might be important, so I asked Glen to have a look."

"You took possible evidence from a crime scene?!"

"Er, I didn't know it was a crime scene when I took it," Fi twisted her hands in her lap and stared at her feet. Her fluffy socks were suddenly extremely interesting.

"I see..." Detective Ledd let a long pause pass as he studied the witch. Fi tried to stop fidgeting under his scrutiny. Eventually, he took a breath and continued.

"Back to the wyrm," Detective Ledd flipped the pages of his notebook as Fi wondered why he didn't use a smartphone to write everything down, "let's see, yes, the wyrm that belonged to Goody Winships, yes?"

Fi nodded.

"So, Goody Winship's pet told you that its master had been killed?"

"Familiar," Madam Mim interjected. Detective Ledd looked at Madam Mim as if he'd forgotten she was there.

"Pardon?"

"Not a pet, a familiar. They are a witch's companion. Familiars have a unique bond with their witch and can often help with their magic."

The detective ignored Mim's clarification. "And how did this wyrm tell you?"

"She spoke to me. In my head."

He blinked three times before asking, "And is this normal?"

"I don't know! I've never had a familiar."

Madam Mim interrupted again, "Familiars can communicate psychically with their witches."

"And how is it that Goody Winship's familiar can speak with you?"

"Don't ask me!"

"We don't fully understand the ways of familiars, but it seems that Ms Blair has a link with Goody's familiar," Madam Mim's voice was calm.

"Hmmm." Detective Ledd wrote in his book again.

"What's this all about?" Fi bristled, her electricity rising under her skin. It was clear that the detective didn't believe her.

The detective looked Fi straight in the eye. "We have reason to believe that Goody Winships died from unnatural causes. We believe someone killed her."

Chapter 18

Fi's mouth gaped open. Her magic dissipated. "So, I was right," she breathed.

The detective arched one eyebrow at her, and she started twisting her hands in her lap again.

"So, Ms Blair, why don't we go back to what you remember about the fete rather than wild theories about cursed broomsticks and psychic familiars?"

"Me? Why would I know anything?"

The detective gave her a long, unblinking stare. And the pieces finally connected in Fi's mind. The police thought she had killed the old witch.

"You think I have something to do with this?" Fi mentally kicked herself. She listened to enough true crime podcasts, and she watched enough cop dramas to know she was sounding either like an idiot or like a suspect. She had to keep her mouth shut.

"Do you?"

"No!"

"Ms Winships' stomach contents included some sort of baked goods…"

"That's hardly surprising, is it? I mean, she was a judge for all the baking competitions, wasn't she?"

"Well, as Ms Winships apparently took part in most of the contests, it seems she didn't actually do any of the tasting…the judges felt that wouldn't be fair. But she did eat something at the fete. Something that might have been a scone with a very particular brand of sugar."

"I didn't see her eat anything at the refreshments tent, she just dropped off a cake." Fi's brain waved a flag through the fog of surprise clouding her mind. "What sort of sugar?"

"The lab confirmed it was Pixie Power Sugar…"

Fi stopped her eyes from going guiltily to her overstocked cupboard of baking supplies, which included several bags of the magical sugar.

"…it's a specialist ingredient, not widely available and not widely used. But you use it in your baking, don't you?"

"Who told you that? I mean," Fi took a breath, "Yes, I use it. It helps with the texture and is always the right amount of sweetness in a recipe…Do I need a lawyer?" Fi's eyes narrowed as she looked at the policeman with sudden suspicion.

"Do you?"

A small part of Fi's brain had kept working in the background because another thought broke through. "You're not accusing me, are you? Or else you'd have arrested me, and we'd be having this conversation at the station."

"I'm not accusing you of anything, Ms Blair. I'm trying to understand more about Goody Winships and her last day, establish a timeline of what she did, who she met and what she ate..."

Madam Mim gave a delicate cough and looked pointedly at the detective. He sighed, "And, because Ms Winships was a, ah, witch, we have the involvement of the Magical Liaison Office here to help with any possible, ah, supernatural aspects of the investigation."

"I didn't know you were with the Magical Liaison Office," Fi looked at the elegant lady.

The sorceress shrugged, "I'm more freelance, but I do work with them and offered to help as Halloween is one of their busier times of year and I was in the area. More specifically, we were wondering if the familiar knew anything..."

Fi took a gulp of coffee, "You want me to talk to the wyrm?"

"If it's not too much trouble."

"I'll see if I can convince her to come down, but she hasn't been very helpful since I brought her home..."

Fi headed upstairs slowly, trying to think. She was sure that Goody hadn't had anything to eat when she was in the refreshments tent, but had she really been paying attention to who she'd served all day? She shook her head and turned her attention to finding the golden wyrm. It didn't take long to find her, as the small animal wasn't hiding. She was curled up in the middle of Fi's bed. The wyrm opened one emerald eye lazily.

Yes?

"It's the police. They want to ask you some questions."

Me?

"That's what I said."

Why?

"They think someone killed Goody Winships."

The wyrm regarded the witch for several long seconds before she stretched. *It's about time someone listened to me.* She stalked past Fi before pausing at the top of the stairs. *Well, are you coming?*

Fi clenched her teeth as she followed the wyrm, telling herself to breathe. It wasn't worth losing her cool over the small creature. She'd be gone to the animal sanctuary soon…maybe Fi could even splash out on a taxi if that would speed things up. The thought gave Fi a small amount of pleasure and she had a small smile on her face as she re-joined D.I. Ledd and Madam Mim in the cosy kitchen.

Cressida planted herself in Fi's vacant chair and sat regally on the padded cushion. Fi unceremoniously picked up the wyrm and took her place.

"You can sit on my lap or on the floor."

The wyrm met Fi's gaze before turning and settling on her lap, ignoring the witch and focusing on the two others in the room. Fi winced as the small animal dug its claws into her leg.

What do they want to know?

Fi repeated the question.

"You said the wyrm told you that Ms Winships was killed?" Fi nodded but kept silent. "How did it know?"

"It is a she; her name's Cressida."

Thank you. The wyrm sounded surprised that Fi had made the distinction. Fi wasn't even sure why she had. The witch shifted uncomfortably as Cressida spoke. *I knew something was wrong before she left the stage. She smelled wrong and her heart was irregular.*

"What does that mean?" The detective pierced Fi with a look that said he didn't believe the witch was telling the truth.

Her heart. She took her medicine that morning, but her heartbeat was irregular later in the day. She didn't seem her usual self and she smelled wrong. Doesn't that idiot understand? She smelled wrong.

Fi edited the response before asking the wyrm a question of her own, "What does that even mean, 'she smelled wrong'?"

I couldn't possibly explain it to a creature that doesn't have the olfactory prowess that I possess. I knew something was amiss. And I knew you humans would be too stupid to realise it. That's when I felt a link with someone - with you - and I knew I had to try to tell someone. She was killed.

Silence fell. It was the longest speech Cressida had made, and Fi could sense the pain and the loneliness contained in it. The wyrm had lost her friend. Fi's hand stroked the golden scales gently.

"Well thank you, ah, Cressida. One more question; can you think of anyone who might have wished to do Goody Winships any harm?"

The wyrm met the detective's gaze and stared. Fi stared too. She mentally listed everyone she knew who had some sort of grudge against Goody. It was a long list. Fi pulled her concentration back to the room. The detective was staring at her politely. She realised he was waiting for her to repeat the wyrm's words. It was the first time she'd been able to tune out the acid voice in her mind.

"Er, sorry, would you mind repeating that Cress? I didn't quite catch it all."

It's Cressida, thank you very much. And I said: Goody Winships was underappreciated and misunderstood. She wanted the best for those around her. Not everyone appreciated her keen eye for detail or her methods, but she lived for Magewell. And some would say that the WWWI would be lost without her.

That was one way of avoiding answering the question because, of course, there was a long list of people who might have wished the old witch harm. But it's not like she was newly unpopular. Fi would be surprised if no one had thought of killing Goody before now given her reputation for meanness and small-mindedness. Even Fi's mum would probably have wished her dead.

Fi struggled to keep her face carefully neutral as the realisation crept across her mind while she translated the wyrm's words. She acknowledged the detective's words of goodbye and a request for her to stay local in case they had more questions for her or her familiar in a sort of daydream. The same five words kept burning through her mind: Her mum hated Goody Winships.

Chapter 19

Fi watched Detective Inspector Ledd and Madam Mim walk down her garden path through the slatted wooden blinds installed in her window. She stepped back out of view as they reached the pavement and turned, discussing something. Net curtains, Fi mused, were much better for spying from your own home. Too late to come to that design decision now though, after she'd already spent a small fortune on custom shutters.

She drummed her fingers nervously on her thigh as she waited for the two figures to leave. She wanted to talk to her mum. In person. It didn't seem right to use the phone when Fi wanted to look her mother straight in those familiar blue sparkling eyes and ask Nell if she'd killed Goody Winships. It seemed a crazy thought. Fi couldn't imagine her mum killing anyone.

Not even when she'd been at her angriest after Fi and Agatha had stolen her car so they could go to a gig in Oxford. The sisters had been grounded for a month and forced to clean the house from top to bottom, including the dusty attic and the ancient cellar. Even then, Fi hadn't thought Nell would kill anyone.

And yet...

And yet the thought was insidious. It had wormed its way into Fi's sub-conscious and was eating away at her. Nell disliked Goody. That was common knowledge. Everyone stepped back instinctively when the two powerful witches met. Their dislike...hatred even...was palpable. But taking the next step and ending a life. Fi shook her head, hating that she was unsure if her mum could commit murder. Surely that should be a simple answer. Is your mum capable of murder? No. As a daughter, how could she even doubt her mum, pillar of the community, Chairwoman of the Omensford branch of the WWWI?

And yet...

She needed to see her mum.

Fi peered out of the window again. She had a notion that alerting the detective to her train of thought by rushing off to see her mother would be a bad idea. Her brow furrowed as she took in the direction that the detective was heading. Uphill. That wasn't unusual. The village centre was up the hill. As was the village hall. And her mum's house... But the officer stopped outside her sister's house. It could be a coincidence, Fi told herself.

The detective opened the gate.

Fi let out an expletive. Did that mean her sister was a suspect or that they were trying to get intel on their mum?

Fi decided to wait. The overwhelming urge to know what was going on compelled her to stay at her post in the small front room, staring out of her window.

What are you doing?

Fi jumped. She had forgotten she wasn't alone. "None of your business," she snapped.

The wyrm jumped up onto the squishy armchair placed by the window and moved her head so she could see out of the wooden slats.

There's no one there.

"No. They're talking to Agatha."

The police?

Fi nodded.

Who's Agatha? Do you think she killed my witch?

"No! She's my sister. I just wish I knew what they were saying to her."

Cressida soon lost interest and sank down onto the soft cushion. She made herself comfortable and sank into a light sleep.

Half an hour later, Detective Ledd closed the gate outside Agatha's house. They walked back towards Fi's cottage. She held her breath, expecting them to walk up to her door and knock again. Her mind played through scenarios of how they might accuse her, arrest her, take her to a cell. They turned down her neighbours' path. Fi exhaled. Of course, they weren't going to arrest her. She was innocent. She grabbed her trench coat and headed out, leaving the small wyrm on her cushion.

With a surreptitious glance at Steve and Glen's house to make sure the detective wasn't still outside, Fi walked briskly to her sister's house. She rang the doorbell, waited half a second, then rang it again.

"Look, I told you," Agatha started as she pulled the door open, "… oh it's you. What do you want?"

"What did they want?"

Agatha looked up and down the street before sighing. "I suppose you'd better come in."

Agatha led the way to her kitchen and filled up the teapot. Fi tapped her fingers on the table impatiently, waiting until they both had hot drinks in front of them before she began to interrogate her sister.

"What did they ask?"

"It was nothing really." Agatha added another spoonful of sugar to her mug. That was three spoons. Fi was counting.

She reached out and put a hand over her sister's. "It's OK Aggy, I'm here."

Agatha stared down at her sister's hand. Fi removed it, aware that she wasn't usually that tactile. Agatha must have sensed something was wrong because she looked up and nodded. "Alright, but then you tell me why you're worried."

Fi agreed. Fair's fair after all.

"That detective was here about half an hour ago. But you must know that as you arrived barely five minutes after he left," Agatha's tone was accusing. Fi stayed silent. With a sigh, Agatha continued, "He wanted to ask about the fete. Did you know that Goody Winships was killed?"

Fi nodded and jumped in quickly as Agatha's eyes narrowed and her lips opened. "They came to see me before speaking to you."

Agatha settled back down. "Well, apparently the world and his wife heard about my little, uh, spat with Goody Winships. He asked if I'd seen her eat or drink anything and if I'd noticed anything out of the ordinary. I think he said they thought she'd been poisoned. He said nature witches knew all about poisons…" Agatha was twisting her hands in her lap, clearly avoiding something big.

"Was that it?" Fi pressed gently.

Agatha's bottom lip wobbled. "Then he…he practically asked me if I'd killed her!"

Fi studied her sister closely, questioning every childhood cruelty that had passed between them, and then she asked the unthinkable question. "Did you?"

"Of course, I bloody didn't! Who do you think I am? I'd never harm another person. I'm a nature witch for goodness' sake! I teach bloody kids. Do you think I'd be able to put up with some of them if I was a killer?!" Agatha's face drained of colour. "Oh! I didn't mean that. I love the kids. I love teaching."

"It's alright, you're allowed to be out of sorts. Someone we know was killed in front of us. It's going to be hard to take in.

Everyone knows you're a brilliant teacher and you love your job."

"Yes," Agatha took a long drink of her sweetened tea, "anyway, they asked about our… 'argument' they called it. Really, it was a heated discussion if anything."

Fi thought back to the altercation, "I think you said she wouldn't get away with it…"

Agatha shot her the sort of look that only big sisters can give. "I might have said something like that. The police seemed to think I did anyway."

"You've got to admit, it doesn't sound good. What did you mean?"

"I only meant that I'd reported it to the other judges. There's no way she could have grown a larger pumpkin than me without a growing spell. I wanted them to investigate it. There're tests you can do, you know? I wanted her to know that she couldn't go on cheating, and she was going to be stripped of her blue ribbon. But I didn't get to say any of that, because she got on her stupid broomstick and now…and now she's dead! She died just after I shouted at her and now everyone thinks I killed her!" Agatha sank her head into her hands and sobbed. "Why did I have to open my big mouth?"

Fi patted her soothingly on the back. "No one who knows you thinks you killed her. You rescue bees out of spiders' webs, for goodness' sake. Everyone knows who Goody's real nemesis was."

Agatha blinked teary eyes up at her sister. "You don't mean…"

Fi nodded and, together, the sisters said the word; "Mum."

Chapter 20

"Fudge!" Fi looked at Agatha. Her sister shrugged, "It's working with the kids, I can't swear any more. But what are we going to do?"

"I have no idea…"

"This is Mum!"

"Yep."

"Mum! She couldn't…"

"Of course not…"

"She wouldn't…"

"No…"

"We should go and see her."

"Yep."

Agatha rushed to the back door and grabbed her broomstick.

"What are you doing?"

Agatha followed Fi's gaze to her hand. "I'm going to Mum's…"

"Why don't we just walk? It's not that far."

"You want to waste precious minutes walking when we could fly there faster?"

Fi swallowed. She wasn't sure she could get on that piece of wood. It wasn't just that she'd been part of a crash at the fete; she'd never been good on broomsticks. Her hands shook as she moved closer. She just didn't seem to get on with anything that wasn't electronic, and even then, she wasn't exactly on the best of terms with things with a circuit board. "What am I going to ride on?"

Agatha looked at her broom again. "It's big enough for two…" She didn't sound sure.

Fi shook her head and stepped back, not trusting the slender wooden broom. Her eyes caught the vacuum cleaner standing behind the kitchen door. She swore and reached for it. She switched it on and felt her power swell through her body. With a flick of her wrist, she sent a careful lick of her power into the vacuum. It lifted off the floor and hovered three inches from the ground. Agatha's eyes boggled out of her face.

"You're going to ride that?!"

"Yep." Fi hopped on more confidently than she felt. The vacuum cleaner dipped slightly, then resumed its floating position just above the easy clean lino flooring of her sister's kitchen. "Easy as riding a broomstick."

Fi angled her vacuum cleaner forward and headed out of the back door. She was almost at the roof when Agatha caught up with her.

"I didn't even know those things could fly."

"I figured it out when I was a teenager and Mum asked me to do the hoovering."

"Alright then, let's go." Agatha leant over her broom and sped over the tiled rooftops of Omensford towards their mother's Bed and Breakfast. Fi followed, turning the power on full. She felt a tug and looked down to see the power cord stuck in a TV aerial. She grimaced and kicked the cable. It came free, sending the witch and her vacuum cleaner spinning before she regained control. She looked over her shoulder to see the aerial bent at a right angle.

"Sorry," she murmured to the owner of the house before hurrying to catch her sister.

Agatha had already dismounted in the back garden. She smoothed down her plaid trousers. Fi landed next to her. The hoover made an angry grinding noise as it sucked up the grass. Fi turned it off.

"You might want to clean that out before you use it indoors…"

Agatha pursed her lips but kept quiet.

"I'll knock, shall I?" Fi wrestled her vacuum cleaner to the back porch next to the wood store and raised her hand to knock.

The door opened with a happy creak before she had a chance to rap on the painted wood.

"Good to see you too," Fi told the house. It opened the door all the way in response and Fi smiled. She loved her magical childhood home. It was just a shame that it came with a large dose of overbearing parental guilt. Speaking of; Nell put down her latest crochet project and peered at the entrance.

"Oh, it's you, is it? I wondered why the house had got the table ready for five."

"Five? It's just me and Aggy."

On cue, Agatha entered the kitchen, pausing to give the door frame a gentle pat.

"How odd. Well, I'll put the kettle on."

Fi sat at the round table while Nell pottered around the large kitchen, selecting matching cups and saucers with delicate cat patterns decorating the rims. She brought these over on an art deco style tray alongside a milk jug and sugar bowl.

"Just got to wait for the leaves to brew."

Fi didn't know anyone else who brewed tea rather than using the ready-made bags that were the staple of normal homes.

"To what do I owe the pleasure?" Nell asked after the tea had brewed to her liking. Five long minutes of silence, through which Fi had fidgeted constantly and Agatha had shot her knowing looks.

"Er, we just wanted to see you about the fete?"

"Oh?"

"Yes," Agatha jumped in, "And ask how you were doing, what with Goody Winships dying and all."

"I see." Nell narrowed her eyes over the patterned ring of her mug. Fi fidgeted and reminded herself that her mum couldn't read minds. "Well, that's kind of you to ask, I'm sure. I'm well enough, thank you. I won't say it wasn't a shock; I thought that witch would outlive us all."

"What do you mean?"

"Goody Winships. I thought she'd always be there. I suppose one gets used to people being there."

"But…you didn't like her."

Nell glared at Fi. "I respected the fellow WWWI Chairwoman."

"Yes, but you didn't like her," Fi persisted, "and you were annoyed she got that lifetime achievement award…"

"What has got into you?"

"The police, they've been asking around. They think she was killed! Poisoned!"

"Oh?" Nell raised one eyebrow and took another sip of tea. She was maddeningly inscrutable.

"Look Mum, everyone knows you were desperate to win the magic contest."

"I was not!"

Fi looked at her elder sister for support.

"Come on Mum, you were worried about losing," Agatha managed before she quailed under Nell's look, "we all were."

"I was not worried about losing to Goody Winships!"

"Then why have you been practicing all hours of the day?"

The look Nell gave her daughter would have withered her prize pumpkin.

"I wanted to be sure of my display. And I am sorry she's dead…I was going to win fair and square and then rub her beaky nose in it!" Nell got her voice back under control, "Anyway, I don't know what's got into you two. Obviously, I don't have anything to do with it, so let's move on."

The doorbell rang. A loud musical chime to the tune of *Danse Macabre*.

"Oh, very funny!" Nell muttered at the house. It had a strange sense of humour. Agatha and Fi exchanged a look as their mother marched to the front door.

"Hello Detective, Madam Mim. I've been expecting you."

Detective Ledd arched an eyebrow. His face wasn't really fashioned for that expression, and he vaguely looked like he might have wind. "Really?"

"My daughters arrived saying you've been questioning everyone in the village and the house set up five seats," she replied, as if that explained everything. "I suppose you'd better come in."

Nell led the way back to the kitchen, where two chairs were still vacant around the large round table. Fi and Agatha tried not to look guilty as Madam Mim and the detective entered. A small smile played around Madam Mim's lips as if she was thoroughly enjoying this. The detective looked irritated.

Detective Ledd sighed, "I suppose you've heard then that we believe Ms Goody Winships died of unnatural causes."

Nell nodded as she poured hot drinks for the newcomers.

"Lovely," Madam Mim took a sip of her tea. "It's so rare that people use leaves nowadays. It's really a lost art."

Nell gave her a warm smile. "I quite agree."

There was a pause as everyone took a sip of their drinks before Nell looked up over her cup. "Poisoning, was it?"

The detective's eyes narrowed. "I can see I'll have to be clearer with the people we're talking to not to share information in an ongoing investigation."

"Well, there you are then."

"What does that mean?" Detective Ledd blinked in confusion.

"I would never have poisoned Goody."

"And why is that?"

"Firstly, Detective Inspector Ledd, I am not a coward and poisoning is, I believe, a coward's choice. Had I wanted to kill her, it would have been a more direct method."

Fi put her head in her hands as her mother carried on, oblivious to the detective's fish-eyed stare at what may be the worst attempt ever of someone attempting to prove their innocence.

"Secondly, if I had wanted to kill Goody Winships, I would not have done so at my own Halloween Fete."

"I thought it was a Tri-village Fete?" The detective was braver than Fi had given him credit for because he met Nell's piercing stare without blinking while he interrupted her.

"It was. But I was…I mean, my village hosted the event. I wanted it to be a success."

"That's true. You said as much at one of the meetings."

"Thank you, Agatha. Yes, I can get you the minutes of our WWWI meetings as proof. I wanted this fete to be a success. I most certainly did not want anyone murdered there! And finally, I wanted to beat Goody Winships in the magic competition, which was due to be held that same day. I needed her alive so I could win fair and square. And that is why I could not possibly have killed the witch."

The detective scribbled furiously in his notebook as he tried to catch up with Nell's logic.

"And what made you so sure you would win?"

Nell looked down her nose at Detective Ledd. "I shall show you."

With that, she stood and glided outside to the garden. The others followed.

Chapter 21

Nell stepped confidently into the middle of the neatly manicured lawn at the back of the house. The low autumn sun added a soft glow to the background and the Japanese maple trees swayed softly in the light breeze, their fire red leaves shimmering expectantly. The detective jumped and twisted in alarm as the house banged its shutters across its windows in preparation.

Nell bent and placed something on the ground before standing and taking a single step backwards. The witch closed her eyes and raised her hands. Fi could feel her mother gathering her power. Whatever this was, it was going to be big.

Nell moved her elegant hands in a complicated pattern. Fi recognised the start of a growth spell. The detective gasped.

Fi followed his gaze. At the spot where her mother had bent down, a small plant started to grow. It twisted and bent delicately as it reached upwards. The small sapling bowed to

Nell before spurting up towards the sky. Its trunk thickened and branches began to sprout, thick with three-pointed green leaves.

The wind picked up and swirled around the tree, rustling the leaves in a magical vortex. One branch bent down, and Nell stepped onto it, lifting her foot delicately as the wind howled. The branch moved around the trunk, lifting Nell into the sky. Her power created a golden aura shining around her, so she looked like an ethereal being atop a tree palace. The tree continued to grow and twist into a perfect umbrella shape. A bonsai tree in full size.

As the witches and the detective watched, the tree's leaves began to turn gold. Not the yellowish sort of gold that you get in autumn, but actual shining metallic gold. They tinkled as they were blown against each other. The soft ringing turned into a full-blown symphony as the air gusted around the tree, with Nell as conductor at the very top of the canopy, her arms waving in time with the music.

The music died away as softly as it had arrived, and the leaves changed colour yet again. This time, they morphed to a bright red. Brighter than the natural maples that lined the garden. These leaves seemed to glow from within. They burned brighter and brighter until they burst into miniature flames. Each one a flickering candle.

The wind grew faster and louder until it was a tornado of magic. The fires grew too into a flaming vortex around the tree. Suddenly, the air stopped moving. With a cascade of sparks, the fire transformed. Fluttering leaves filled the air.

They moved around softly, circling the magical tree trunk, speeding up with each completed circuit. The small hairs on Fi's arms stood on end at the immense power her mother was channelling.

Agatha gasped. Fi frowned before letting out her own gasp. The leaves fluttering around the tree were beautiful orange butterflies, each one the size of a maple leaf. The cloud of butterflies whirled higher and higher until they were hovering above the tree in a perfect ball formation, continuing to turn. Fi's eyes drifted downwards to her mother.

"The tree!" Fi spoke without thinking.

Before their eyes, the tree branches withered, drying up and shrinking. Nell stood on the treetop. Her hands had stopped moving and her eyes were closed in concentration as the butterflies continued to flutter in a cloud around her. The sound of wood splintering cracked through the air. The tree began to collapse in on itself.

A cloud of fine powder filled the garden as the tree disintegrated. The spectators covered their eyes as the dust cloud expanded.

"Mum!" Fi shouted, taking a step forward. Madam Mim laid a hand on her shoulder and smiled down. Was this part of the trick?

A gust of wind pushed the dust outwards and then up into the sky and away. Fi looked at the spot where the tree had been. Her eyes tracked upwards. Nell glided down to the floor, supported by the cloud of butterflies. She descended gracefully, with a small, satisfied smile playing around her lips. As the heels of her buttoned up boots touched the grass, the butterflies glowed brighter and brighter until they exploded with a flash of sparks. Fi covered her eyes at the flash of light.

Applause sounded behind her. Madam Mim clapped enthusiastically. Agatha, Fi and the detective joined in. Nell kept her smile small, but the satisfaction in her eyes grew.

"That was, ah…" the detective started.

Nell nodded serenely.

"Very well done," gushed Madam Mim, "the play on the tree of life and the four seasons in one brief moment. I don't think I've ever seen a better interpretation of the fleetingness of life itself."

This time, Nell's nod was one of respect. "That means a lot coming from you, Madam Mim."

Fi realised she had been standing with her mouth open since her mum had floated down on a flutter of butterflies. "Wow," she managed. She hadn't realised her mother had so much power. Judging by the similar guppy look on Agatha's face, she hadn't known what their mum was capable of either.

"I hope that shows you I had no motive to kill Goody Winships."

"Wha–"

Nell interrupted Detective Ledd before he could ask the question. "I wanted to perform this feat of magic at the fete, to prove that I was the better witch. Goody could brew a potion but she… well, let me simply say that I am confident that I would have won best trick had the day played out the way I intended."

The detective nodded dumbly. Fi didn't think he knew what he was doing. That was probably the first time he had seen magic first hand outside of Royal Variety performances. Mundane humans, those without magic, tended to ignore it or resent it until they needed something from supernatural beings. It was harder to ignore it in a registered magical village, though. And even harder when you'd just seen a tree grow and die in less than thirty minutes.

Madam Mim gave that small smile again. "I think we're done here. I will treasure the memory of that illusion and thank you for the tea." She placed one slim hand on the small of the detective's back and ushered him around the house to the side gate.

Nell turned to her daughters and crossed her arms. She raised one eyebrow. "You'll have to find another suspect to badger. Now, are you staying for dinner?"

Chapter 22

Fi parked the vacuum cleaner back at Agatha's house and kissed her niece goodnight. One didn't turn down a home cooked roast dinner from Nell Blair and, knowing that her mother would have overcooked as always, Agatha had called Neville and Bea over.

Bea also acted as the perfect distraction for Nell so she didn't criticise her daughters constantly, although Nell had made veiled hints that it would be nice if the family moved back in. The house had been on its best behaviour too, making sure the chairs were comfortable and the fire was blazing against the autumn chill as night fell.

Overall, Fi thought, as she wished her sister goodnight and headed over to her own small cottage down the hill, it had been a pleasant evening. And her mother hadn't seemed too upset about being accused of murder, although Fi noticed that the portions of apple crumble and custard that she and Agatha received were notably smaller than everyone else's.

But knowing that her mum was innocent didn't help. The detective might be overawed by Nell's magical powers today, but she was still an easy suspect. She had a grudge and the power to kill Goody Winships and hide it. Fi's mind tumbled round and round. If it wasn't her mum, who was it?

Her phone buzzed. She picked up the bulky Nokia. A message from Maxi.

Just read the report from Madam Mim. Sorry I can't be there - tarfangtula infestation in Camden. Stay safe x

She texted back that she was fine and made a note to buy herself a new phone before she let herself into her cottage and headed straight upstairs to bed. She was exhausted.

Well, did you find anything out?

Fi let out a scream. She had forgotten the wyrm was staying in her house and, as she looked into the accusing emerald eyes, she made a silent vow to call up the animal sanctuary in the morning.

"I found out my Mum is practically a sorcerer, and she isn't the killer."

She isn't? Are you sure? She was Goody's biggest rival... Cressida sounded sceptical.

"She didn't do it, OK? Now I am tired. It's been a long day and I'm going to bed."

What about finding the killer?

"It'll have to wait until tomorrow!" Fi stormed upstairs and got ready for bed. She was lying under the thick duvet, drifting off to sleep, when her eyes snapped open.

"The bins!" Fi let out a string of curse words. Tomorrow was bin day, and she'd already forgotten the last collection day, so the recycling was practically overflowing. She couldn't leave it for another two weeks. With another curse, she crawled out of bed and shrugged on a warm dressing gown.

The air was thick with a coming storm, and her powers moved restlessly under her skin in anticipation. She pulled her dressing gown closer as the wind whipped around her. She continued muttering under her breath as she trekked down to the end of her long garden to grab the bins.

A noise sounded in the quiet night. Fi stopped. The crunch of a boot on gravel came again. Footsteps. Why did she keep the bins at the end of the garden? She made a vow to move the bin store to the side of the house before the next collection. A rustling from next door. She gathered her power to her hands and called out.

"Is anyone there?" She hated that her voice came out nervous instead of powerful. She was the daughter of Nell Blair for goddess' sake. With a cough to clear her throat, Fi tried again, "Who's there?"

A small, soft whimpering sounded from the other side of the fence. Was there a hurt animal? Fi wished she'd brought a torch. She moved towards the fence and stood on an old tree stump to peer over.

The whimper turned into a snuffle. "It's just me, sorry if I scared you."

Fi looked down into Steve's wet eyes.

"Steve? What are you doing down there?"

Steve stood, took out a handkerchief, and blew his nose as quietly as he could. "I didn't want Glen to see me like this."

Fi screwed up her face; she was pretty sure that Glen's superhuman hearing meant he could hear someone crying at the end of their garden. "But why are you crying? What's wrong?"

Steve looked away, staring at the opposite fence. Fi knew he wasn't really seeing the lichen-covered wooden panelling.

"Steve, please, what's wrong?" Fi reached her hand tentatively over the fence and rested it on Steve's arm.

"They think I ki…killed her!" he howled.

Fi looked around. If Steve had wanted to keep things quiet, there was no question that he'd just drawn attention to their sleepy street. "How about a cup of hot chocolate at mine?"

Steve met Fi's concerned blue eyes and nodded once. Fi stepped off her stump and moved away from the fence. Steve put his hands on top of the panel and leapt over in a single bound. The wood shook at the unexpected pressure but stayed upright. It wasn't fair how athletic werewolves were. Fi led the way back to her kitchen.

Once inside, she warmed the milk in a small saucepan before mixing in the chocolate powder and melting in a couple of squares of dark chocolate for extra decadence. There wasn't any point in having comfort food if it wasn't bad for you. She sprinkled in a mix of spices automatically before expertly tipping the hot chocolate into two bowl-sized mugs.

Steve sniffed the cup. "Cinnamon?" he murmured appreciatively before taking a sip and letting out a contented sigh.

Fi smiled, glad that he was calming down. She itched to ask him what had happened and tapped her fingers against her thigh to stop herself from blurting out any insensitive questions. He stayed quiet, staring into the rich brown drink for long minutes. Fi forced herself to sip her own hot chocolate and try to savour the velvety texture and sweet taste instead of watching the werewolf.

"I can't believe they think I killed her!" Steve finally blurted out, his eyes flashing with anger.

Good, thought Fi, he had moved past sad. "Goody Winships? Why would anyone think you killed her?"

He sighed, the anger leaving his face as quickly as it had arrived. "That detective said that she'd eaten some sort of baked goods on the day…on the day…at the Halloween Fete."

"That doesn't mean you killed her!" Even to Fi, that argument sounded weak.

"They must have spoken to someone because they knew that I made most of the baked goods for sale, except the scones of course," he added with a smile at Fi, "thanks for that by the way, I'm not sure my oven would have coped if I'd had to batch cook them as well." Fi waved away his thanks and motioned for him to continue.

"And Goody would have had to try my cake as she was one of the judges…"

"So would every other judge and none of them died!" Fi thought for a moment. "Although, the detective told me that she didn't eat anything from the tents in case there was a conflict of interest."

"That's what Glen said," a look of pride stole onto Steve's face, and he lit up as he spoke of his partner. "But then the detective asked how I'd felt when she beat me in the baking competition," Steve's bottom lip started to wobble.

"I mean, I was disappointed, of course, but it was just a baking competition. I would never even think of killing anyone! And then the detective said it was in my nature…"

Fi's jaw dropped and she reached out to hold Steve's hand. She had never known a more sensitive man. Anger blazed through her, and she fought to control the sudden surge of energy that swept through her body. How dare anyone suspect this gentle giant? How dare a human use outdated prejudices against him?

"Ouch!" Steve withdrew his hand quickly. Fi shook her own hand as if that could help dissipate her power. She closed her eyes and took a deep breath. It was too late. Power crackled from her and jolted towards the sockets in the small kitchen. The light bulb exploded, raining glass onto the round table.

Fi sighed and found the matches she always kept in one of the kitchen drawers. She lit a pillar candle and apologised to Steve.

"Sorry, it happens sometimes when I get too emotional…"

Steve looked around with wide eyes but kept silent. It wasn't like he hadn't seen her power before.

"I'll just check the fuse box…" Fi lit another candle and scurried out of the door to the fuse box in the hall. She checked. Dammit. She had blown the fuse. Again. She grabbed a spare and changed it with the practised ease of someone who had to change a fuse about once every three months. The lights came back on. Except the one in the kitchen. Fi dug out a spare bulb and changed it quickly.

Steve was looking amused now. Which was a step up from crying. "Madam Mim had a similar reaction, but she was a bit more controlled."

"Really?"

"She said that if the detective was going to be prejudiced about dealing with magical beings, she was going to have to submit a report to the Magical Liaison Office. He calmed down after that, which was just as well. Glen was about to shift and bite his head off!"

"So, he admitted you're not a likely suspect?"

"We-ell, he said I wasn't to leave town. As if I could leave; Zadie's got her recorder recital coming up at school this week." Steve turned his face to the window, looking fondly at his own house.

Fi winced. She had heard Zadie practising her recorder songs. If the werewolf was enthusing about watching her perform, he was either deaf or a great dad.

Steve sighed again. "I suppose it was all a bit much for me. I mean, I've never been accused of murder before! And Glen's been so angry about it all, I didn't want to get upset in front of him. Silly of me, really. Anyway, thanks for the hot chocolate, I'd better go. I've still got to put the bins out and Glen'll be wondering where I've got to." Steve headed outside into the chill night air. He turned on the threshold and swept Fi into a huge hug. "Thanks for listening."

Something pricked in Fi's memory. "Glen said you bought potions from Goody."

Steve nodded. "They were meant to help with the, ah, effects of the full moon, but I don't know if they ever really worked. I mean, we still have to get a babysitter every month. Thanks again."

He leapt the fence and Fi heard the familiar trundle of a wheelie bin being moved along gravel. Fi swore. The bins! Pulling her dressing gown around her, she headed back out into the night.

Chapter 23

Fi was curled up in bed in her comfiest, brushed cotton pyjamas and fluffiest bedsocks when she heard the first rumble of thunder crash through the night. She smiled. She loved storms. The raw, unbridled power of nature thrilled her.

She felt the prickle on her scalp as her hair rose in response to the electrical charge in the air. The covers landed in an untidy heap on the floor as she ran to the window and flung it open. She whooped as a flash of lightning filled the dark night sky. Her power itched through her fingers. A thought whispered in her mind; she could ride the storm.

She wasn't living under her mother's roof anymore. She could run into the garden and let wave after wave of lightning bolts flood through her, drawing her own power up into the atmosphere. It was tempting, oh so tempting.

The last time she'd channelled a storm had been the time she'd felt most in control of her power. She wrapped her arms around herself, clamping down the electricity that threatened to rise through her body and explode into the night. She took half a step away from the sash window before stopping. The memory of the dark July night flashed through her mind. It was the first, and only, time she had felt right rather than resenting her gift.

***

She had been in control, dancing on the wet grass, embracing the wildness of the tempest. The wind whipped round her, causing her soaked cotton nightie to press against her skin. She raised her hands to the sky, allowing her power to flow free into the night sky. Her skin tingled with electricity. She laughed and released her magic in joyous sparks of magic.

As the storm crashed overhead, Fi found she could almost direct the lightning. She released a blast of energy into the sky and the storm responded, sending lightning back to her. She screamed as the bolt hit her. Her heart pounded against her chest, but it hadn't hurt, more been a shock to her system, a power overload. She laughed at the overwhelming intensity, but it wasn't an experience she wanted to repeat.

Instead, she focused on using her magic to send the lighting to specific spots in the garden. It was easier to direct it to trees and taller structures. The smell of charred wood filled her nostrils, mixing with the scent of fresh rain.

She'd felt she could control anything…up until she couldn't. Her hand aimed for the house's chimney. Lightning struck and the house slammed its shutters in response. She stared, guilt piling up inside. Fi turned back to the garden, better to stay away from using the house for her magic practice. Then she heard her mother shout from the window.

In her surprise, electricity shot from her hands towards the window. She'd heard the scream. A combined shriek from her own mouth and her mother's voice merged with the rolling thunder. With electricity still coursing through her body, Fi ran into the house to her mother's room to find Nell curled on the floor, staring at the shutter hanging from one hinge, flames flickering even as the heavy rain fought to put it out.

Fi tried to apologise. She reached out to her mother. But the electricity was still there. It shot through her arm and into Nell. Her mother had cried out in pain. Fi moved forward, but Nell lifted one manicured hand and stopped her. Fi flinched from the hurt and, worse, the fear, she had seen in her mother's eyes. But her mother recovered quickly, retreating behind her haughty persona.

"You will never try to control a storm again. It's too dangerous."

Fi was too upset and too ashamed to argue. And worse, her mother was right. She was dangerous. She couldn't control her power. She didn't need to exacerbate it with a storm.

***

Fi turned back to her window with a heavy weight inside her chest. Best not to even think about riding the storm. She could damage something, or worse, hurt someone again.

She folded her arms and rested against the windowsill, trying to ignore the prickling under her skin as her power sought for release. She clamped her lips together and rubbed the back of her calf with one sock-covered foot, as if that would relieve the building pressure.

She wouldn't give in and use her power. But she could still watch. She stayed there until the storm blew itself out and the sky turned from black to the ghostly grey of the early hours of the morning. Only then did she head back to sleep.

Chapter 24

Fi stretched out and opened her eyes. She screamed. An inch away from her face, the small golden wyrm was staring at her with large emerald eyes. Goddess, would she ever get used to having a pet in her house?

Good, you're awake.

"We need to set some boundaries," Fi grumbled as her heart slowed back to its usual pace. "Like no staring at me while I'm asleep. It's creepy."

The small animal continued to look at her. Fi sighed and stretched.

"I suppose you want breakfast. What do you even eat?"

I prefer Welsh coal, or a well-cooked steak will do.

"Er…" Fi reached for her smartphone on autopilot before she remembered that she'd fried it. She tried to remember what she had in the house. "How about some, er, burnt toast?"

The wyrm looked at her.

"Or I might have some bacon I could fry up…"

Cressida flicked her tail and jumped off the bed. *Bacon will be acceptable.* She disappeared down the stairs.

Fi rubbed her eyes and headed to the shower. Seven minutes later, she felt ready to start the day. She selected a podcast on her phone and perused her clothes. Normally, she wore black tops with leggings or jeans to give off a smart vibe when she took calls for her job. Today she wasn't logging in to work. Her hands drifted towards a red sweater dress. Might as well wear her favourite colour. It might even bring her luck in the job search. She pulled on a pair of leggings and chunky socks. Then she paused and opened up her laptop. She searched for the wyrm sanctuary. Fi cursed to herself; they didn't open until later. She quickly inputted the phone number into her phone before joining Cressida downstairs.

What took you so long?

"Nothing," Fi said too quickly.

The wyrm looked up from the bowls she had been eyeing on the draining board. Fi decided to at least try and look like she was in control of something in her life before the reptile broke anything else. She put her hands on her hips and stared down at the small animal.

"Right, let's clear some things up."

More boundaries?

"Exactly. No more breaking my stuff! And my bedroom is out of bounds, especially in the mornings!"

Is that all? The wyrm blinked up at Fi innocently.

"Er, yes, I suppose it is."

Agreed. And you will help me find Goody Winships' killer.

"Wait, what?"

I overheard you and the werewolf yesterday. It's clear that the authorities are bumbling imbeciles flailing around. You will help me.

Privately, Fi had come to a similar conclusion about Detective Ledd. If he could even think that Steve might harm a witch intentionally, then he didn't have many leads in the investigation. But there was such a thing as pride, and Fi didn't intend to side with the disagreeable wyrm. "But I don't know the first thing about police work…"

What are you listening to?

Fi glanced down at her phone. "It's a true crime podcast. They look at crimes and talk through how the criminals were caught."

And you listen to a lot of these pod… casts?

"I suppose so."

And you don't think that any of the people that the police suspect killed my witch?

"The prime suspects seem to be my family and neighbours!"

Then you should want to prove their innocence…and your own.

Cressida had a point. Fi kept quiet, pursing her lips. The wyrm knew she had won.

I take my bacon charred.

Fi muttered to herself as she fried the meat. She buttered herself some bread, might as well go all the way if she was going to have an unhealthy breakfast, and loaded it with crispy bacon and ketchup. She found an old plate and put the remaining burnt bacon on that and took it over to the table. Cressida sat expectantly on one of the painted chairs.

"Animals eat on the floor." Fi set the plate down with a clatter on the slate floor before taking a seat at the table.

Cressida narrowed her eyes before acquiescing and jumping gracefully down to the ground. Fi watched the wyrm as she ate, noticing how the reptile wolfed her food. With a guilty jolt, Fi realised she must have been starving. The witch wasn't used to taking care of anyone else. Better to get Cressida to the animal sanctuary as soon as possible before she got hurt. To distract herself from her poor caretaking abilities, Fi drummed her fingers on the table and thought back to Goody Winships.

"Where would I even start?"

The wyrm's eyes glittered as she met Fi's gaze. *Start with her home.*

Fi finished the rest of her sandwich in silence. It wasn't a bad idea. And the wyrm was probably homesick. After washing up the dishes, Fi pulled on her converse trainers and opened the door. It was raining. The sort of continuous drizzle that only seemed to occur in Britain. It didn't look too bad, but Fi knew from experience that she would end up soaked. She pulled on her trench coat and grabbed an umbrella.

She would have looked chic if the umbrella hadn't been in the shape of a ladybird with gigantic, disproportioned eyes bulging from the top. Thank you for last year's Christmas present, Bea. Fi knew that her sister had been behind the ugly purchase, and she couldn't throw away a gift from her niece. But she was planning her revenge. There was a particularly awful garden gnome she had spotted in the garden centre that would be perfect for her sister.

Cressida jumped up onto Fi's shoulders and curled up as tightly as she could against the autumn drizzle. Fi loosened her coat. The dragon-like reptile was like a furnace around her neck. She adjusted the umbrella and stepped outside.

Fi trudged towards the bus stop. They waited in silence until Fi spotted her sister leaving her house. She waved, and Agatha paused and stared.

"Oh, hello. What are you smiling about?"

"Nothing," There was a garden gnome in her sister's future…the most hideous one she could find.

"OK…is everything alright?" Agatha peered around, trying to see beyond her sister.

"Yes, I'm off to Magewell. When the bus decides to turn up."

"You're in luck, I was going that way anyway to do a big shop. You can come with me."

Fi scrambled around for a good reason not to accept her sister's offer. "Thanks, but I wanted to go into the village rather than to the supermarket…"

"No problem."

"Don't you have work today?"

Agatha shook her head. "It's my day off. What's wrong? Do you want a lift or not?"

Fi squared her shoulders and accepted the offer of help. "I do, thanks."

It looked like Agatha was joining their trip to Magewell.

Chapter 25

Once they were in the confined space of the car, Agatha turned to Fi.

"What are you going to Magewell for?"

"Oh, I just…need to buy a new phone."

Her sister frowned. "Why not use the shop in the village? That's where you always go, I thought they gave you a discount."

Fi scowled; she didn't need her sister reminding her that she broke her phones often enough to be the only customer on a loyalty programme at the local phone shop.

"So, you want me to drop you on the High Street?"

Fi turned to Cressida for help.

She lived near the fields.

Fi huffed a sigh at the wyrm. "Really helpful."

"What is going on?"

Fi sighed again and told her.

Agatha was silent for a long moment as the gardening programme on the radio droned on about the best watering schedule for petunias.

"I'm coming with you."

"What?"

"You don't expect me to let my little sister go to a murder house on her own, do you?"

"It's not a murder house! And I'm going alone."

Agatha let out a noise like a horse snorting. "You are not. You need me. What if you get into trouble? What would I tell Mum if you got hurt?"

"Everything revolves around Mum, doesn't it?"

"Yes."

There was a moment of silence, which Fi broke by snorting out a laugh. Their mother was a dominant figure in both their lives and often it did feel like she was the centre of the universe. Agatha chuckled too.

"Fine, come along."

They found the house an hour later, hampered by the fact that the only passenger in the car who knew where the dead witch had lived was an animal who had never had to direct anyone to the house by road.

Agatha parked in front of a higgledy thatched cottage that might have been an original Tudor framed building. Cressida scratched at the car door, eager to be back at her house. Fi let her out and smiled at the wyrm's exuberance as she darted to the cottage. Agatha stood beside the car and folded her arms.

"Looks like Goody was the living embodiment of the witch stereotype. The only thing missing is the cage for the children."

Fi rolled her eyes.

"How are we going to get in?"

"Maybe the door's unlocked?"

The sisters walked up to the front door. It was locked.

"I'll try round the back. You see if she has a spare key hidden somewhere," Fi headed off to the back door. Once there, she took out her phone and looked around furtively before dialling the number she had saved earlier.

"Hello, you're through to Haernson's Dragon Ranch. Dylan speaking, how can I help you?" A lilting Welsh voice answered the phone.

"Er, I've sort of inherited a wyrm…"

"And you're finding it a bit much to look after?"

"Yes, yes, exactly."

"Right-o, well, we offer an owner's course right here in our own sanctuary. I can send you over the details if you like. Accommodation and meals are all included over the weekend. Our next course is…" Fi heard pages turning. Did nobody use their phone to organise their calendar? "…the first weekend of December."

"That's very kind of you, but, er, the thing is…"

The male on the end of the phone sighed, "You want us to rehome it for you?"

"Please," Fi said weakly.

"Let me speak to Owain and I'll call you back later in the week to arrange a collection time. What's the best number to get you on?"

Fi gave her name and number before the voice on the end wished her "Ta-rah." and hung up.

Fi turned and saw Cressida watching her with knowing eyes and a sulky look. Fi twirled her hair nervously.

There's a key under the mat in the shed.

The wyrm flounced off to wait by the stable door at the back of the house.

"Wait, Cressida..." Fi tailed off. Her stomach twisted uncomfortably. The wyrm had obviously heard the call. But Cressida knew this arrangement was only temporary, didn't she? With a sigh and a side helping of guilt, Fi went to the shed. Under the old straw mat was indeed a key to the back door. She opened it. The wyrm ignored the witch as she ran inside. Fi followed and navigated her way to the front door to let her sister in.

Agatha raised her eyebrows questioningly.

"Spare key," Fi said.

"What are we looking for?"

"No idea." Fi crossed her arms and made her way into the lounge. The room was full of floral chintzy furniture and homemade crafts. It looked like Goody had practiced a lot for all her entries into the craft competitions.

"Cressida?" Fi called, looking around for the wyrm.

Agatha went to the kitchen and started opening drawers. Fi decided to see if Cressida had gone upstairs. She hesitated by the door to Goody's bedroom. It was such a personal space; it seemed like an intrusion to go in. A small whimper sounded from the room. Well, Fi reasoned, she was already intruding, she might as well explore everywhere.

Fi stepped inside. Goody had decorated the room in rich greens and golds, with a large four poster bed dominating the floor. Cressida perched on a mahogany nightstand, staring at a picture of Goody holding the small wyrm and smiling. The wyrm wasn't crying. Fi didn't even know if reptiles could cry. She knelt on the worn carpet.

"Oh Cressida, I am so sorry for your loss."

No, you're not.

Fi paused. The wyrm had a point. "Well, I didn't really know Goody. I get the feeling not many people did. But she was obviously important to you."

She was my witch…and now she's left me alone in the world.

"She didn't choose to leave…"

The golden wyrm's eyes flashed. *No, she didn't. And I won't rest until her killer is brought to justice.*

"And I'll help you."

You just want to be rid of me.

Fi opened her mouth to protest then stopped and decided she owed the wyrm honesty. "I'm sorry you overheard that. I promised to help you find the killer and I will. I keep my promises." Fi placed a hand on the animal's warm back. The wyrm nodded. "What are we looking for?"

I don't know.

Well, that was clear. Fi tried not to sigh as she followed the creature around the house. They checked the guest room, which was filled with the bare necessities, should anyone come to stay. Fi guessed Goody didn't have a lot of visitors. Fi wandered into the small bathroom. She nodded appreciatively at the cast iron roll top bath before perusing the cupboards. There were a lot of pill bottles.

"Do you know what these are for?" Fi called to the wyrm. No reply. Fi took out her phone and snapped a few pictures of the labels. That was something she could research online later.

Next, Fi and Cressida made their way to Goody's study. Cressida sniffed around the stacked cauldrons and baskets of herbs that marked the witch's trade. Agatha joined them and picked up a glass bottle.

"A most potent curse," Agatha read. "Are we sure she didn't kill herself accidentally? Just kidding", she added hastily as smoke started curling from the wyrm's nostrils. "What's this one? An amorous aphrodisiac…"

Fi ignored her sister and selected books at random from the tightly packed bookshelves. She squinted at the small handwriting in a Diary of a Witch.

A heavy knocking sounded on the front door. Fi looked up, startled. A crash of glass came from behind Fi. She turned to see Agatha looking guilty and the aphrodisiac potion smashed on the floor. The knock came again.

Chapter 26

The sisters looked at each other.

"Someone must have noticed the car outside."

"I suppose we should answer it?"

"Well, go on then?"

"Why me?" hissed Fi.

"It was your idea to come here!"

"It was Cressida's idea," Fi retorted, but her heart wasn't in it. Her sister had won the argument, and they both knew it. Fi made her way to the door and took in the shadowy figure through the glass as the knock sounded again.

She opened it, trying to exude confidence. "Hello?"

An elderly woman with a round face blinked up at her. "Oh hello, I was just passing, and I thought I saw movement in Goody's house. Can I help with anything?"

"Er…"

"I'm Margaret, Goody's friend. We met in the St John's tent I think, but I didn't catch your name?"

Fi recognised the small woman now. "I'm Fi and this is Agatha. We're looking after Goody's wyrm…she's been a bit restless so we thought that we could bring her back here and maybe get a few of her things."

"Oh, right, well that's alright then. Would you like to come over for a spot of tea? I'm only down the street."

"Thank you…"

"Watch out for the fumes on those bottles," Margaret peered past Fi to Agatha. "Are you alright, love?"

Fi turned. Agatha was fanning herself with her hand.

"What? Oh, um, yes. Yes, thank you. Quite alright. Yes. Just a bit, er, hot."

"You don't look well at all…" the older witch's gaze dropped to the floor. She squinted. "…Is that Goody's love potion? Oh dear, well best come round to mine and I'll see if I can brew up something to help."

Fi went to help her sister, who was now even pinker and more flustered. Fi took her arm gently and propelled her out of the front door, following the older lady to her bungalow.

"We're here now," Fi said reassuringly.

Agatha's eyes had glazed over. Fi sped up their pace through the garden, which was filled with a riot of blooming flowers.

"Come in, come in. Goody always makes…made her potions very potent. I think some camomile will help and, yes, lavender for good measure…” Margaret carried on naming herbs as she mixed a tea for Agatha.

“Oh,” Agatha uttered a single word. Fi frowned with concern and moved her sister out of the kitchen and onto a sage green sofa in a tidy living room.

Once she had finished, the witch brought a small blue teapot through from the kitchen and placed it on a low table. “That’ll be about five minutes for it to get to full strength. Can I get you anything to drink, dear?”

Fi asked for a black coffee with sugar and set a timer on her phone before resuming fanning Agatha, who was now moaning slightly and pressing her thighs together. Fi tried not to look. It was too embarrassing to see her sister hot and bothered.

Margaret returned to the room with two mugs and handed one to Fi. Fi blew on her coffee to cool it down and drank. She looked around the room and floundered for something to say as they both waited for the timer to sound. The living room was neat and tidy, with porcelain flowers lining the mantelpiece above a coal-effect gas fire. The sunlight reflecting off the mirror above the fireplace lent the pink room a cheery air.

A patch of orange caught Fi’s eye out of the window. “You’ve got a lovely garden.”

Margaret’s eyes lit up. “Thank you. It’s rather a passion of mine.”

“I’m surprised to see so many flowers, everything in Mum’s garden seems to have faded for the winter.”

"Well, between us witches, I'll admit to a little magical help. I love the flowers and, of course, it helps the bees too."

The timer rang loudly, at odds with the quiet sitting room.

"The tea's ready," Margaret stood and poured the contents of the small teapot into a flower-patterned mug. She tilted her head to one side and considered the prone witch on the sofa. "We should get her seated upright, so she doesn't choke."

Fi manhandled her sister into a seated position. She ignored the low moan Agatha emitted as Fi gripped her shoulders. Margaret offered the teacup to Agatha.

"Drink this dearie."

Agatha tried to lift her hands, but they had curled into tight balls as the lustful sensations flowed through her. The sunlight bounced off a light sheen of sweat on her forehead.

With a sigh, Fi took the cup and brought it to her sister's lips. Agatha drank slowly but Fi persisted until the cup was finished.

"I'll just refresh the pot," Margaret offered, and she bustled back into the kitchen.

Agatha blinked and took in the rose-coloured wallpaper. She turned to her sister. "Where are we?"

"In Margaret's house. She found us at Goody's old place and offered to make you an antidote for the potion."

"Oh, I would never presume to be able to offer an antidote to one of Goody's potions, but I think this will take the edge off as it were." Margaret made her way back into the room with a refilled teapot.

"Thank you," murmured Agatha. Fi looked at her sister. Agatha's cheeks were still very pink.

"How well did you know Goody?" Fi asked, making polite conversation.

"Oh, we've known each other for years. I helped out you know with organising things for the WWWI...it felt like we did everything together really...it won't be the same without her..."

"Can you think of anyone who wanted to hurt her?"

Margaret took a long drink of her tea, peering at Fiona with sharp black eyes, "I got on well with Goody. Everyone respected her here in Magewell." Fi opened her mouth to apologise but the witch carried on. "She was respected but not, I think, well-liked. She had a very directive manner, and she liked things done her way. If she were here, she'd tell you it was the right way. People resented her for that, and for her power. She was a very accomplished witch."

"So, no one in particular would want her dead then?"

Margaret tilted her head to one side. "Her biggest rival was Nell Blair..."

"I know, that's our Mum."

"Ah," the witch looked embarrassed. "I think the next batch is about ready now," she gestured to the blue teapot.

Fi poured for her sister, not trusting Agatha to pour without spilling tea everywhere. Her hands were shaking. Agatha practically downed the second cup. She still looked hot and there was a strange glint in her eye, but she didn't seem to be sweating anymore.

Agatha looked around the room expectantly. "What happened to the wyrm?"

Fi swore then apologised to Margaret, "I completely forgot about her! She's probably still at the house! Sorry Margaret, we'd better go." Fi raced to the front door.

Agatha followed more slowly, as if she was thinking carefully about every step. Margaret waved them off from the door and watched as they headed back to Goody's house.

"It's a shame we had to leave. Did you see her garden? Beautiful rhododendrons, I wonder how she's got them to bloom so late." Agatha's tone was wistful.

"She said she used magic." Fi was brusque, she had little interest in gardening. "Come on, who knows what trouble that wyrm's gotten into now!"

Chapter 27

The wyrm was, in fact, waiting politely next to Agatha's pick-up truck, her tail curled neatly around her golden feet. Fi narrowed her eyes suspiciously.

While you were off getting tea, I conducted a thorough search of the house.

"What did you find?"

Nothing of interest.

"Great."

"Mmmm," Agatha moaned as she leaned on the car.

"Are you Goody's next of kin?" a sharp voice broke through Fi's grumbling. Fi turned and found herself face to face with a witch's hat. The thick brim was battered and worn, the point flopped to one side and the once black material had faded to a dark brown, but it was clearly a witch's hat. Fi thought she saw a sticky stain halfway up, covered with dust. She lowered her gaze to take in the woman below the hat who had a crinkled, brown face much like an overripe apple.

"What? No."

"Oh. I thought you might have been. Why are you parked outside her house, then?"

Fi forced herself to take a deep breath. "We're, I'm, looking after her wyrm. We came back to pick some things up."

"Right, right. You were close then? I suppose someone had to like her."

"You know what I'd like…" Agatha swayed slightly against the car door.

"Not really…" Fi pulled her sister to one side and opened the car for Agatha to get in. Her sister just stood there, a glassy look in her eyes. Fi paused, one hand resting on the car door. The lady's words sunk in, and she turned back. "So, you didn't like her then?"

The lady snorted. Her green eyes glinted behind horn-rimmed glasses as she readjusted her woollen coat and shifted in her sensible brown leather shoes. "No one liked Goody Winships. The witch was a tyrant."

The lady spat on the pavement. Fi stepped back unconsciously.

"What do you mean?"

"I mean that everything had to be done her way or no way. She was obsessed with the bloody Institute and bloody Magewell. She wasn't even born here; did you know that? She acted like a queen, but she was a newcomer. Everyone was too afraid of her to ever argue. Except for me, o' course."

"You argued?"

"Oh, I did it to annoy her most of the time, but she got what was coming to her!"

Fi gasped. Did the wrinkled lady really mean what she had just said?

The lady noticed Fi's reaction. "What? Just because she's dead means I have to be nice about her? I tells the truth, and the truth is that Goody Winships were a nasty piece of work and we're all better off without her or my name's not Olga Merchant."

"Is it?"

"Is what?"

"Your name. Is it Olga Merchant?"

"Of course it is. Are you simple?"

Fi shook her head.

"Did you know that she even left her cottage to the village to be preserved as a museum? I ask you, the nerve of that witch! Well, you can bet they won't accept it! My daughter's a solicitor and she said that the terms aren't binding. That cottage'll be sold to line the council's pockets, you mark my words."

"Do you know what else was in the will?"

The woman scratched her whiskery chin. "No, I can't say as I do. But you can bet it won't be anything to benefit Magewell that's for sure. She wouldn't do anything that wasn't on her terms. I don't know why that one put up with her for so long." Olga jerked her head towards Margaret's house. "The goddess knows I wouldn't have!"

The woman poked Fi in the ribs with a wicked smile and walked away towards the town centre, her canvas shopping bag flapping slightly in the wind.

Fi stared after the woman in the brown loafers. Had she just met the killer? Agatha swayed slightly, bumping into Fi's shoulder.

"Maybe I should drive," Fi offered, bringing her attention back to her sister. Agatha nodded and handed over her slouchy handbag. That was when Fi knew her sister really wasn't well. Fi only had a provisional licence, and Agatha was proud of her pick-up truck. Fi dug around inside the bag and pulled out a huge bunch of keys. She found the key fob for the truck and helped her sister inside. Cressida jumped onto the back seat.

As Fi started up the powerful car, Agatha let out a groan that was somewhere between pleasure and pain. The effects of the potion were still affecting her senses.

Fi pulled out then slammed her foot on the brake as another car drove past. Shaking, she clicked on the indicator and tried again, checking the mirrors three times before she drove away from the curve.

Out of the village, on the narrow country lanes, her grip on the steering wheel tightened as she spotted a tractor bearing down on them. She swerved into a passing place and overshot so the car was partially in the hedge. On the flatbed, the huge pumpkin bumped against the side. The tractor driver gave her a cheery wave as he passed. She swore and reversed, scudding a tyre against a tree stump. She glanced over at her sister, who grasped the side of her seat with both hands. Fi grimaced and pulled out again, overcorrecting and almost driving the pick-up into a ditch.

"Oh goddess," Agatha moaned, her eyes closed as the car crawled along. Her face was flushed.

"Don't worry, I'll get you home." Fi forced the car into third gear and accelerated down the country lanes that connected the villages, using the large vehicle to get right of way over smaller cars.

Her knuckles were white by the time she parked on her sister's paved driveway. Even the supersized pumpkin still on the flatbed made it back in one piece, despite the bumpy roads.

Fi helped Agatha out of the car and supported her to the front door. She fumbled with the keys, trying to keep Agatha upright when the door opened.

Neville peered at them from behind his glasses, "Aggy! Glad you're back. Did you get the chocolate orange biscuits from the shop?"

"We didn't make it to the shop," Fi muttered.

"Wha...?" Agatha interrupted Neville's question was by launching herself at her husband, crushing him against the door frame with her kiss.

Fi scrunched her face up in a mix of disgust and horror. She chucked Agatha's handbag through the open door into the hall and practically ran away from the house. There were some things a sister shouldn't have to witness.

Chapter 28

Where are we going?

Fi hugged herself, still disturbed by her sister's lust. "I need a drink." Having spoken her thoughts out loud, she sped up. She didn't fancy drinking alone, so there was only one place to go: The Witch's Brew.

Fi ignored the sign showing a Hollywood version of a witch, complete with green skin and a wart on the end of her nose. Fi didn't blame the local pub for rebranding when Omensford had gained protected supernatural status; it had been decades ago after all, but she was surprised her mum and the rest of the WWWI had allowed such a blatant stereotype of witch culture.

She waved at the two old blokes sitting on a bench outside and nursing their pints; Jack and Jeremy raised their glasses to her.

"Alright love?"

"You look like you've seen a ghost!"

"Something much worse," Fi muttered as she pushed open the door, went straight to the bar and ordered a pint of lager.

"Sure thing, Fi, and can I interest you in some of our new bar snacks?"

Fi looked at the menu. "Wizard's fingers?"

Sounds awful.

"Spiced sausages, perfect for a winter's day…hey is that a wyrm?"

Fi looked down at the floor, where Cressida snaked out her long neck and flicking her forked tongue. "She is."

I'm parched.

"Cool, would you mind dropping in with it the next time we get a coach load of tourists here?"

"Er, I'm not sure she's sticking around that lo-ong. Hey!" Fi glanced down. The wyrm had bumped the back of her knees, causing her to knock into the bar. She rubbed her elbow and pursed her lips.

"So how about those wizard's fingers?"

"No thanks, Brian, but, er, can I get some water for the wyrm?"

Sparkling mineral water.

"Er, sparkling water please."

Brian got the drink and turned back to restocking the small fridges behind the bar. Fi sipped her beer and looked around, taking in the patrons. Seeing a familiar friendly face, she smiled and walked over to one of the small tables under a string of old-fashioned lightbulbs.

"Hey Liv, can I join you?"

"Of course, pull up a chair."

Fi sank into an upholstered chair and made herself comfortable. Cressida hopped up on the bench next to Liv and sat regally.

"Your patients driven you to day drinking?"

Liv curved her red lips, "I've got a free afternoon and thought I'd treat myself," she let out a small sigh, "this morning's session was particularly difficult, and I've got a long night ahead."

"I don't know how you do it."

"Just doing my job."

"Yeah, but how can you go into people's dreams, it's…" Fi sought for the word, "…icky."

Liv laughed, "You don't want me to sift through your dreams then!"

Fi joined in the laughter and shook her head before taking a drink.

Liv raised one eyebrow. "So, how's it going?"

"Is that a shrink question?"

"It's a friend question," Liv took a long drink.

The thing about having a therapist for a friend, Fi thought, is that they are uncommonly good at holding silences. Fi sifted through the events of the past couple of days while

Brian brought a toasted panini and chips to the table. Liv took a bite of the grilled sandwich and regarded Fi with her chestnut brown eyes.

"We-ell it's been…eventful. Do you want to hear something crazy that happened to Agatha?"

"Always, but I'm interested in you, too."

"I did have a question for you." Fi unlocked her phone and scrolled through her pictures, deflecting attention away from herself. She missed Liv's wry smile as she helped herself to a crisp chip. "Do you know what these pills are for?"

Liv leaned forward and took the phone with interest before shaking her head. "I could hazard a guess, but those sorts of medicines aren't really my area. I think that one's for something to do with heart problems, but I don't know for sure."

"What sort of heart problem?" Fi pushed Liv for an answer, but the therapist was resolute.

"Unless it's a sleeping pill, I wouldn't want to say. You'd be better off asking a medical doctor. Why are you asking?"

Fi put her phone away and grabbed another chip from the bowl that Liv had placed thoughtfully in the centre of the table.

"I'm trying to work out who wanted Goody Winships dead."

Liv arched one perfect eyebrow. "Isn't that the police's job?"

"Normally, but…it seems like almost everyone I know is on the list of suspects, including me. I want to clear our names."

"I see…and how are you finding the time to do this sleuthing?"

Fi swallowed. As usual, her friend had got right to the point. "I, uh, lost my job. Again. I know, I know, I'm a failure and I should be looking for a job instead of chasing after hunches. You don't have to say anything."

"I didn't say anything! And if I was going to say something, it was going to be that it's nice to see the glint back in your eyes. I haven't seen that Blair glimmer in a long time."

Fi uncrossed her arms and tilted her head as she looked at her friend. She had always thought she was destined for a job in computers, ever since she'd built her first PC at the age of ten. She loved computers. And she got a lot of satisfaction from tracking down the problems that came across her desk and fixing them…but…she hadn't honestly loved her job in a long time. About the time the computers started blowing up more frequently as a result of her power surges.

She remembered the first work computer she'd caused to short out. She'd had the radio on. The newsreader was talking about a dragon destroying Cardiff Castle. She'd stopped to listen and wondered if it was fake news. Supernaturals didn't often make the news, but dragons? They were extinct.

She had paused in her typing to listen when the call had come in. No doubt it would be someone who just needed to restart their computers. Frustrated by the interruption, her power had jumped to the surface and, with a crackling fizzle, the laptop's screen had turned blank. Maybe her subconscious had been trying to tell her something…

"I do like solving problems," she said slowly.

"I know."

Fi tapped her fingers on the side of her pint glass as she thought. There was one way she could get the truth, but would her friend go for it? Liv hated speaking about the other side of her powers, but Fi felt she had to try. "I don't suppose you could… you know…help with this one. If I could just speak to Goody, I know I could figure it out."

Liv's eyes instantly hardened. "That's not how it works, and you know it."

"OK, OK, forget I asked."

"I'd better go. Have another drink on me." Liv threw some money down onto the table and stalked out.

Fi watched her go, annoyed that she had even mentioned the other part of her friend's gift.

What's going on?

"I'm an idiot and I asked too much of her. I should have known she wouldn't go beyond the dream realm and into the never-ending dream of death." Fi took a long drink. Now she was going to have to apologise and she was still no closer to solving Goody's murder.

What are you going to do now?

Fi shook her head to clear it, popped another chip into her mouth and chewed thoughtfully. "Good question."

Chapter 29

Fi finished typing, leant back on her padded office chair and stretched her arms towards the ceiling.

Did you find anything?

She shook her head and reached out to absentmindedly stroke the agitated wyrm. Since she'd returned home yesterday after buying the cheapest smartphone she could find in the local phone shop, Fi had decided to approach the problem in a way that felt more natural to her. More logical than running around chasing every villager.

She'd spent the afternoon creating a virtual workspace to capture her thoughts about the case. Initially, Cressida had been sceptical, but once Fi had started to fill out the space and create links, the small wyrm's head had bobbed around with excitement as she dictated her thoughts for Fi to add to the virtual board.

At the top was a list of unanswered questions that synced with a list on Fi's own phone via the cloud. There were a lot of them. Fi rubbed her eyes and headed to the kitchen for a coffee. That was the problem with projects; Fi got drawn into them and lost track of time. She hadn't gone to bed until three a.m., and she was feeling the effects. As she brewed the beans, she drummed her fingers on the cool worktop.

If only she could figure out those medications. An internet search had brought up too many possibilities to be useful. But it felt like an answer that was within her grasp instead of the bigger question of whodunnit.

Absentmindedly, she pulled out her phone and checked it. No messages. Why wasn't Liv replying to her *I'm sorry* texts? She shouldn't have asked her friend to go beyond the veil and try to find Goody's spirit. Not that she'd actually asked that. But still, she shouldn't have hinted at it.

With a sigh, she returned to the pills. If only she could speak to a doctor. A thought whispered in her mind. She pulled out her phone and called the local surgery. She was in luck. They had an appointment today. She checked her phone. In ten minutes. She accepted the appointment and quickly transferred her coffee into a travel mug before heading to the door.

"Oomf." She tripped over Cressida.

Where are we going?

"*We* are not going anywhere. *I* am going to the doctors to ask about heart medication. You can stay here and stay out of trouble."

What am I going to do while you're gone?

Fi gave an exasperated sigh before turning on her large flat screen TV. "Here, you can watch something on this. What do you like?" Fi flicked through channels, trying to gauge the wyrm's reactions.

She left two minutes later with Cressida sat down in front of a cosy detective drama. As soon as she was out of the house, Fi started running.

The doctors' surgery was on the other side of the village and Fi arrived breathless and dishevelled. Two minutes late. She knew because the chirpy receptionist behind the desk informed her she was late as she checked in. Fi grimaced and settled down in the waiting room. Of course, the one time she was late, the doctor would be running on time. She wriggled in her seat, the plastic coating on the padded chairs squeaking under her butt. The plastic might be practical for the odd accident, but it wasn't comfortable.

She smiled as always at the doctor's name on the notice board; Dr De'ath. It was a long running joke in the village; Fi and every other child had called him Dr Death since she was in school, but he was really a nice doctor, and he never minded the extra call outs to magical accidents that were a staple of the Omensford community.

Fi drummed her fingers against her thighs in an absent-minded rhythm as she waited to be called, the lie she had thought up at home running through her head. A male voice crackled through the intercom.

"Ms Blair please."

Fi jumped to her feet and walked towards the familiar pine door, her hand still tapping against her thigh. She knocked twice just below Dr De'ath's nameplate, then pushed the door ajar before stopping in her tracks. A tall man with a head of dark hair was seated in the worn swivel chair, clicking at the ten-year-old computer in front of him.

"Come in, sit down."

Fi couldn't move. The doctor sitting at the chipboard desk wasn't the sixty-year-old GP that Fi had been seeing since her teens.

"Please, come in," the doctor stopped clicking the mouse and turned, raising familiar deep chocolate eyes to Fi. His lips curved into a smile as he recognised her.

"I should go."

"Not at all, please take a seat."

Fi swallowed and moved forward, closing the door behind her. She took a seat next to the desk and stared at her hands.

"So, what brings you here today?"

She swallowed again, the lie drying up in her mouth. She licked her lips nervously. She flicked her eyes to his face and looked down again. He was watching her, his expression a mix of compassion and good-natured curiosity. She squirmed in her chair, feeling like a worm abusing the trust of this caring doctor.

"I was expecting Dr Death, I mean De'ath," Fi's face heated.

"That's me." Fi frowned and Mort smiled at her confusion, "It's my father too; he's not been well, and he's asked me to look after his surgery."

"Oh," Fi flailed around for something to say, "I didn't know he had a son."

"I lived with my mother up north," he shrugged, "but you're not here to discuss my family history. What can I do for you?"

Fi swallowed again, "Heart."

"I'm sorry?"

"It's my heart; it's a bit weak. I wondered if I should be on some medication for it?"

"Hmmm," the doctor turned back to the computer, "there's nothing in your notes about a weak heart…let me have a listen." He grabbed a stethoscope from the table and placed the two buds in his ears, "If you could face the wall and lift your top…" Fi's face was now beetroot red as she lifted her sweater and faced the wall, "…it'll be a bit cold I'm afraid."

She inhaled sharply as the cold metal touched her skin. She told herself it was just the shock of the stethoscope.

"Hmmm, and now if I could hear from the front…"

Fi turned back around and stared at the ceiling. This was the worst plan in the history of plans.

"OK, thank you." Fi made the mistake of looking into Mort's eyes. She was glad he wasn't listening to her chest anymore because her heart skipped a beat. "Your heart rate is a little fast, but nothing to worry about. Is there something else you want to tell me?"

Fi took a deep breath in. She'd been found out. "Can you tell me why someone would take Flecainide?"

The doctor's brows drew together. "Why do you want to know about beta blockers?"

Fi coughed and pulled out her phone. "I found them in Goody's medicine cabinet. I wondered if they might have something to do with how she was killed."

He frowned again, "A weak heart might make someone more susceptible to oleander poisoning, but the police were quite clear the poison was in something she ate…"

Fi whipped out her phone noted down the name of the poison, "Oleander…"

Mort paled. "I shouldn't have said that."

"Don't worry. My lips are sealed." He glanced at her lips. Fi licked them nervously, "I mean, I won't say anything. How do you know what poison was used?"

"I asked the detective to keep me informed after what happened at the fete…why are you asking about her?" Mort's tone turned suspicious.

"I'm just trying to find out more so I can convince the detective I didn't kill her."

"Did you kill her?"

"No!"

"Only joking, you don't seem like the killing sort."

"You haven't seen me play Fortnite," Fi joked before shifting in her seat. It probably wasn't the best time to be making jokes.

"Fortnite?"

"It's an online shoot-em-up tower defence game, you can play as different characters and there are different modes. I'm enjoying the creative world at the moment..." she trailed off. Not everyone was into online gaming.

"Sounds fun. Not as good as Mario Kart, but maybe you can teach me some time."

"You play videogames?" Fi couldn't keep the scepticism from her voice.

"You'd be surprised what I can do." The doctor's voice was almost like a caress. Fi didn't think she could blush any darker red.

"Sure," she squeaked.

The doctor looked over at the clock on the wall. "I'm afraid that's our time for today. Any more questions Detective Blair?"

Fi laughed and shook her head. "Not right now, but I know who to call if I do."

"Here," he scribbled something on a pad of paper and handed it to her, "in case you have any more medical emergencies."

She took the piece of paper and let herself out of the small office. She was halfway home before his words caught up to her brain. The doctor had asked her to teach him Fortnite. That was almost the same as a date...unless she was misreading him. She wasn't always great at reading emotions. Just ask her ex. That was the reason he'd left. Well, one of them. Her not being romantic was another biggie. She shook her head, physically forcing herself away from thinking of Li.

Instead, she pulled out her phone and searched for oleander poison, careful to choose incognito mode so her search history wouldn't get her in trouble. It would not look good if one of the first searches on her new phone was for the same poison that killed Goody.

The symptoms matched what she had witnessed at Goody's death, apart from the broomstick crash, but she didn't learn much more except that it was only fatal in large doses or if a person had underlying health problems, like a weak heart. She snorted. She had learned that much from the doctor.

Fi glanced down at the paper in her hand. There, scrawled across the yellow page, was a phone number. Fi stopped mid-stride. The doctor had given her his mobile number. So, he did like her. She transferred it to her phone, feeling the grin spread across her face as she strolled home.

Once she was in the door, she headed straight to her computer. Cressida blinked awake as Fi floated past. The wyrm slunk out of her comfortable chair and padded after the witch to her home office.

How did it go?

"Hmm? Oh, the doctors. Yeah, great. Really great."

Cressida frowned. *Why are you grinning? Did you find out who did it?*

"What? No, I mean, but I found out what killed her. She was definitely poisoned."

How does that help? Who did it?

Chapter 30

Fi forced her thoughts away from attractive doctors and phone numbers and what that might mean. The wyrm regarded her with a suspicious expression on her reptilian face. Instead, Fi talked out loud as she clicked through the notes she had made on her virtual workspace.

"If this was a crime novel, they'd ask who benefits from her death. But Goody apparently left everything to Magewell itself, which means everyone benefitted…or no one did." Fi shook her head. "And she didn't have any children, so no motive around disinheritance there. So, if the motive isn't money…focus on the means…

"The police think the poison was in something that Goody ate…she had a scone, apparently…from the refreshments stall. That rules out Steve. Let's assume it was one of my scones - that's what the police think - and the poison wasn't in that…which means it was in something else…"

What are you talking about? Cressida stared up at Fi from the floor.

"…so, what else do you have with scones? Butter? Or more likely jam and cream…the cream was from the supermarket so unlikely to be tampered with but…but the jam was homemade."

Her power crackled around her fingers as she clicked faster and faster. Strands of hair lifted from her head as the static built.

But…

"Not now Cressida! I'm on a roll. I just…need…to find…aha!" Fi punched the air in excitement. A bolt of electricity shot out of her fist into the ceiling. Fi gazed up guiltily at the black patch in the plaster.

At least the light hadn't been on. She ought to buy shares in a bulb company the rate she went through lightbulbs. Her head shot back to the computer. Thankfully, it hadn't been impacted by her outburst. Tentatively, she reached out her hand and guided the cursor back to the profile on screen.

"Thank you, Sita, for posting every single picture online."

She scrolled through pictures of the Junior Witches' Brigade collision and oversized vegetables. She flicked past the picture of Harris' humorous parsnip. And there, on Sita's social media feed, in between a close up of the huge owlbear and a picture of the judges standing underneath a banner that proclaimed 'Tarts for sale', was a jar of homemade strawberry jam, stamped with a picture of a familiar out-of-shape witch's hat.

Chapter 31

Fi grabbed her coat and headed straight back outside, with Cressida in tow.

What is it? Where are you going?

"Back to Magewell! I think I know who killed Goody!" Fi spotted the red bus coming down the road. She dodged between two parked cars and ran for the bus stop.

The driver chuckled as she climbed in, panting. "In a hurry, are you?"

Fi didn't have an answer. She swiped her card on the contactless payment device and headed for a quiet seat at the back.

"You'll need a lead for that animal!" the driver shouted after them.

Fi waved and picked up the wyrm. Cressida looked around at the public transport and curled her lip at a piece of gum stuck on the back of the chair in front of them.

I have to tell you... Fi ignored the wyrm and plugged in her earphones and folded her arms. Her fingers and feet tapped along to an unheard rhythm in her mind.

The bus trip to Magewell from Omensford was normally a forty-minute drive, filled with peaceful countryside and picturesque villages. It took in such sights as Dragon's Hill, an ancient long barrow said to be a tomb and, if you were of a fanciful bent, you could even see a standing stone said to mark the entrance to the otherworld. Fi saw none of this.

Her mind was crammed with a single-minded determination to confront the killer. It had briefly occurred to the witch to call the police, but she knew her theory rested on what a true crime podcast would call 'circumstantial evidence' and she had a feeling that any actual evidence might have already been destroyed. After all, the killer was a witch. And witches were many things, but stupid they were not.

A not insignificant part of her also wanted to confront the killer herself. If she had thought about it, she might have recognised the same adrenaline buzz she normally got from completing a particularly complex level on one of her videogames. Except better. Much better. Her foot tapped faster. She couldn't contain her nervous energy.

Just as she thought she might explode from the tension, the bus pulled up outside Magewell's Post Office. Fi made her way to the front before the bus even stopped and she swayed as it jolted to a halt. With a small smile at the driver, she rushed out of the vehicle, Cressida at her heels.

She started walking before realising she had no idea where she was going. She pulled out her phone and got up a map, squinting at the screen as she searched for the road. She found it easily and yomped off in that direction. While she walked, she frantically tapped a name into her smartphone. The witch she was looking for wasn't on social media, but Fi found a list of WWWI members on the Magewell branch website, and that gave her enough to find a house number. She already knew the street.

What are we doing here?

Fi ignored the wyrm as she paused outside of the house, panting after her quick march. Now she was here, she was less sure. It looked like an airy bungalow from the outside, but who knew what horrors lurked within. Fi noted the strawberry beds in the front lawn. This was a witch who liked gardening all year round and, judging by the size of her fruits, wasn't afraid to use growing spells.

"We're going to catch a killer," Fi said, deciding. The witch refastened her trench coat and headed for the door. She reached her hand up to ring the doorbell. The front door opened the split second before she pushed the bell.

"Hello there. You again, is it? Better come in I s'pose," the older witch shuffled into her house, leaving Fi to follow. Fi wasn't sure exactly how this sort of confrontation was supposed to go, but she was certain it wasn't meant to go like this.

"If I'm not back in ten minutes, you run to Margaret's house and tell her I'm in trouble," Fi whispered out of the side of her mouth before she entered, closing the door behind her.

You do realise that you are the only witch I can communicate with? The wyrm stopped talking. Fi was already inside. Cressida stared at the shut door. *Oh right, just leave me out here in the cold then. Fine. I see. I'll just wait here like a dog shall I? And if you get into trouble, I'll bark twice to let them know little Fi is lost down a well.* The wyrm grumbled before trying to find a comfortable spot on the doormat.

Chapter 32

Fi barely took in the seventies orange hallway as she followed the older lady deeper into the bungalow. She was suddenly acutely conscious of the sweat patches under her arms after marching from the bus stop, or was it because she was now in a house with a killer? Her eyes darted to the door. Why had she allowed Olga to shut it? She loosened her coat and tried to look intimidating.

"So, what's so important you came haring up here and racing to my door?" Olga leant against her kitchen cupboard, arms folded and stared Fi down. Even in her housecoat and sheepskin slippers, the old witch looked formidable.

Fi swallowed. She hadn't expected to be confronted so confidently by an old lady. She allowed her power to rise under her skin, feeling the tingle as it leapt to be free. It gave her the confidence to speak. "Er, you made the jam for the Halloween Fete?"

The older witch nodded slowly. "That I did." She observed Fi with gimlet eyes. "But somehow, I don't think you're here to ask for the recipe…"

"No, well, yes, in a way." Fi took a deep breath and gathered her power to her hands, ready to deflect whatever Olga might do when she was accused. "You killed Goody Winships."

Olga's jaw dropped. "What makes you think that? And you can stop drawing power. If I was going to hurt you, I'd have done it already."

"You made the jam…and you didn't like Goody…" Fi mumbled, as she shook off her hands. This was not going how she expected at all.

The older lady shook her head and shot Fi a sympathetic look that cut like a dagger, "Oh dear. That's the basis of your reasoning, is it?" then she laughed. Actually laughed. A proper belly shaking chuckle that rocked up the witch's body.

"I don't see what's so funny…"

Olga wiped away a tear. "No, I don't s'pose you do. Come on and sit down." She gestured to a chair and put the kettle on, still chortling away.

The older witch placed two mugs on the table with enough force that the tea sloshed over the sides before taking her own seat. "Dear me, that was the best laugh I've had in a long while. You should of seen you face when you was accusin' me!"

Fi crossed her arms defensively and looked at the floor.

"Now don't as be takin' it so pers'nly. You've done me the world of good you have." Fi started to speak but Olga cut her off, "So I will take the time to explain to you why you're wrong."

"That's good of you."

"I said not to be takin' it pers'nly! Now tis no secret that I weren't a fan of her lady Winships. That's the truth, so I can see as how you thought I might want to kill her, but, truth be told, she did things no one else would for this village and for the WWWI." Sensing Fi was about to interrupt, the witch held up a hand. "Now I didn't agree with what she did or how she went about it, and I told her so many a time to her face. And I won't say I'm sorry she's gone, 'cos I ain't. But I didn't kill her."

Fi chewed her lip as she considered this while Olga drank her tea. "But you made the jam for the fete."

"You said that already, and I don't deny it. But I don't see as what it has to do with anything."

"Goody Winships was poisoned."

"Was she now? I didn't know that. Bad way to go. Mind you, a broomstick crash isn't a good way to go either. Me, I'm hopin' I slips off quietly in my sleep."

"She had a scone at the fete…" Fi persisted.

"And?"

"And we were serving scones with jam and cream; the cream was bought from the supermarket, but the jam was homemade. Your jam."

The witch laughed again. "So, you thought I poisoned the jam! Well, that is rich! And even if I could somehow manage to poison only a tiny bit of jam instead of the whole jar, I tell you this. Goody didn't have jam on her scones, she didn't like the stuff. No, she had thunder and lightnin'"

"What?"

"Thunder and lightning." Olga exaggerated her pronunciation as if Fi was stupid and seeing Fi's blank expression, she elaborated, "Cream and honey."

"Oh." Fi's face heated. What an idiot she'd been to think she could solve a murder investigation on her own.

"Oh indeed. You can drink your tea now; I haven't poisoned it."

Fi flushed more deeply and looked down at the floor. She stood; her confidence gone along with the adrenaline buzz. "No thank you, I think I'd better go. Sorry, I…" she stopped. How exactly did one apologise for thinking someone was a murderer? She twisted her hands together and stared at her shoes.

Olga escorted Fi to the door companionably. "No, no, thank ye, I'll have a story to tell the ladies at the next meeting, I will," and still chuckling to herself, Olga shut the door.

Fi scuffed her shoe on the path and shoved her hands into her coat pockets. Great, now she was going to be the laughingstock of Magewell. And it would probably get back to her mum. Just great.

Back are you?

"Yep," Fi sighed, her shoulders slumped. "Looks like Goody didn't even have jam on her scones…"

I could have told you that.

Fi stared at the wyrm. "Then why did you let me run off and accuse an innocent old lady?!"

Olga is hardly what I would call an innocent old lady.

Fi thought for a moment. "Well, no," she conceded, "but you could have warned me!"

I tried to.

"Oh. Sorry."

You didn't listen to me. How can you help if you can't even accept aid when it's offered?

"I said sorry. I'll listen to you from now on." Fi held her hand over her heart as the wyrm opened her mouth to speak again. "I swear."

Cressida nodded. *Apology accepted. Now what?* The reptile scrambled up Fi's body and perched on her shoulders.

"Back home I suppose." Fi stuck her hands into the deep pockets of her trench coat and walked slowly back to the bus stop where they had to wait forty-five minutes for the next bus.

Chapter 33

Fi gazed out of the window this time, but she still didn't see any of the famed Cotswold gently rolling scenery as it passed the window. She wasn't a detective. Not even an amateur one, and she'd wasted too much time focusing on trying to find a killer instead of looking at her own problems. Inwardly, she berated herself for jumping to stupid conclusions and then accusing someone. Her face heated just thinking about it. A flashing blue and red light caught her attention briefly as the bus wound into Omensford. They were the real police. She should leave it to them and stick to looking for another job.

She stepped down from the bus and considered going to the pub for a quick drink. She was at the door before her dwindling bank balance loomed in her mind. The cheque she hadn't yet cashed from her sister was still at her house. Would it really be so bad to take the money? After all, Agatha always wanted to help.

"Alright love?" Jack, or possibly Jeremy called from the bench.

Fi nodded, not really paying attention.

"You coming or going?" the other man added, and they both snorted with laughter.

"Well, whatever you do, don't go down Hill Road. The police are crawling all over the place down there."

Fi stopped and stared at them. That was where she lived. Fi pulled out her phone. There were three missed calls and a message from Maxi.

Just at the Office and heard they're about to make an arrest on the Halloween killer. Exciting stuff! x

Chapter 34

On the other side of town, Agatha redialled her sister's number with mounting frustration. Where was she? Agatha picked up the trowel and dug viciously into her flowerbed as she eyed the street. Gardening was the best excuse she could come up with for spying on the police, and there was always weeding to do. She breathed in the calming scent of freshly turned earth for a moment before she stood and made a show of stretching her back to get a better view of the street.

Fi clearly wasn't home. The police were still knocking on her door. Maybe she should go and talk to them, or would that just make them suspicious? She frowned, unsure of the best course of action, and she hated being unsure almost as much as she hated not being able to help.

Neville came up behind Agatha and wrapped his arms around her.

"Not now Neville! Can't you see something serious is happening?"

Neville peered over her shoulder. "Why are there police at your sister's house?"

"I don't know. What if she's done something stupid?"

Her unspoken thoughts whispered; what if she's the murderer? She shook her head. Surely not. Fi played those violent videogames but that didn't mean she could kill someone, or did it mean she was more capable of murder? Agatha shook her head again. Not her baby sister who could barely look after herself.

"Give Fi some credit. She can take care of herself." Neville startled her with his insight, so close to what she had been thinking.

Agatha spun round. "She might think she can, but she always needs someone to pick up after her. Like the time she blew up the computer lab at school; I had to pull the fire alarm so no one would get suspicious. She's so proud and independent, but she still needs my help!"

Agatha made her decision. She had to support her little sister, whatever she'd done. She dialled again. The call finally connected on the fourth ring.

"Fi! Thank goodness you answered. Where are you?"

"What? I'm outside the pub in town. Why?"

"Stay where you are. Don't come home. I'm coming to get you."

"Why? Agatha what is going on?"

But Agatha had already hung up. Speed was of the essence; she was sure of it. After all, marked police cars and detectives didn't turn up at someone's door for a nice cup of tea. She considered her broomstick but decided that a car would be less conspicuous.

"Look after Bea, I'm going to get to the bottom of this." Agatha gave Neville a peck on the cheek and walked as nonchalantly as she could to the dented pick-up truck. She didn't want to raise any suspicions. She was just a regular person, getting into their car. She let out a faux curse word when she noticed her enormous pumpkin still rested in the tailgate. Nothing for it now, it would have to stay there. There wasn't time to unload it. Agatha reversed out of the drive and headed towards town. She eyed the police officers milling around outside her sister's house through her rear-view mirror and kept driving.

Once out of view of the police, Agatha accelerated sharply. She rounded the corner at an unsafe speed. The huge pumpkin in the back rolled dangerously to one side before the vehicle came to a halt on the double yellow lines of the high street.

Agatha rolled down the window. "Get in!"

"What is going on?"

"The police are outside your house!"

Fi swallowed and twisted as if she could see the police approaching. She climbed in, holding the door open for the small wyrm to follow her into the cab. Agatha gunned the accelerator and sped out of Omensford.

"Where are we going?" Fi peered out of the window at the darkening grey sky.

"I don't know. I'm trying to keep you safe."

"I don't need your help!"

Agatha swerved at her sister's sudden outburst. The pumpkin thudded against the tailgate. She regained control. "You might think you can do everything yourself and pride yourself on being Miss Independent but really, you're just selfish!"

"What?!"

"You heard me! You take, take, take and you never think about what anyone else might need. You don't think that Mum is lonely and might want some company in her house, all you can see is that it will look like you've failed. Selfish."

"That's rich coming from you!"

"What does that mean?"

"It means you always have to save everyone, don't you? Even if they haven't asked for help, you just swoop in like some goddess forsaken angel to save them. I didn't ask for your help!"

"Well, you clearly need it! The police are at your house!" Agatha took a deep breath and asked the question she dreaded knowing the answer to. "...Look you didn't do it, did you?"

"How can you even ask me that?!"

"Well...you know, you're...you."

"What's that meant to mean?"

"You don't exactly march to the same beat as everyone else…"

"Liking computers and spending time alone does not make me a murderer!"

"You haven't said you didn't do it…"

She's got a point…

"Of course, I didn't bloody do it. I didn't even know what bloody oleander was until the doctor let it slip."

"Oleander?"

"That was the poison someone used to kill her, it was in her stomach. I looked it up online and all it said was that it can be made from azaleas…I don't even know what a bloody azalea is."

"It's another name for a rhododendron," said Agatha, her eyes not leaving the road.

Fi stared at her sister before regaining her voice. "We have to turn the car around now!"

"What? Why?"

"I know who killed Goody Winships!"

Chapter 35

Fi grabbed onto the chair as Agatha executed a dangerous U-turn on the B-road and sped back in the opposite direction. They were silent for long minutes as BBC Radio 4 filled the car with a talk show that debated whether supernaturals were a benefit or a blight to society. Agatha switched it off.

"Look, I'm sorry OK."

"No, I'm sorry. You're right, I am selfish."

Agatha shot her a smile. "I guess I can be a bit overbearing."

Fi grinned back. "Want to help me clear my name and catch a murderer?"

"What else are sisters for?"

Agatha jerked the car to a halt. The pumpkin in the flatbed slammed into the back of the cabin. "Are you sure this is the right place?" she asked dubiously.

"This time I'm positive." Fi rubbed her neck. Now wasn't the time to bring up the possibility of whiplash.

Are you sure?

Fi slammed the car door shut; her pride pricked by the wyrm's lack of faith in her. "I'm sure. Come on."

The sisters approached the bungalow warily. Cressida slunk close to Fi's feet, almost tripping her. Nothing moved in the muggy afternoon air. The thunderclouds in the sky hung fat and heavy with rain. Fi knocked on the door. No answer. She motioned to the side with her head.

"Let's try round the back."

Agatha gulped and nodded. Fi pushed the cast iron side gate. It opened with a loud creak. So much for the element of surprise. The back garden was more of a field, filled with flowers of all kinds.

Agatha nudged Fi in the side and pointed at a busy plant covered with orange flowers. "Rhododendrons."

Fi tapped her fingers against her thighs and scanned the flower beds. She walked forward. The path was paved, and Fi's converse trainers were silent on the paving slabs.

Slap. Slap. Fi turned. Her sister's crocs were smacking against her feet as she moved.

"Sorry," Agatha mouthed.

Fi screwed up her face in frustration and kept going as Agatha slipped the shoes off her feet. The path opened onto rows and rows of white wooden beehives. At the very end of one of the rows, a figure clothed in white beekeeper's garb moved between the hives. The beekeeper must have known the sisters were there, but they kept on working.

Fi stepped forward until she was in front of the beekeeper.

Chapter 36

"I'm surprised you're here." Margaret was unnaturally calm as she scraped honey into a large container and replaced the honeycomb carefully into her hive. "I don't suppose I can interest you in some honey?"

"Is that the same honey you used to poison Goody Winships?"

"Figured that out, did you?"

At Fi's ankles, Cressida hissed.

"Why did you do it? You two were so close…"

"Close? If you mean she relied on me for every little task in the WI, took credit for my ideas and treated me like dirt, then yes, we were close." Bitterness seeped into Margaret's voice as the honey oozed off the scraper in her hand.

"You've been her friend for years…"

"Yes, and this year she was going to be presented with a lifetime service award by Madam Mim no less! A lifetime service award! She did nothing! I organised everything for the

WWWI, for her, and she didn't even blink when she got the letter. She bragged about it to everyone. To me!" Margaret's voice was punctuated by spittle as she ranted, "She thought it was her due. I saw her thank you speech you know, no recognition of me, no thank you for dutiful little Margaret. That's when I realised, I couldn't be anyone as long as she was there."

"You had to realise you'd be found out?"

Margaret shrugged. "Actually, I thought I'd get away with it. Everyone hated that cow; everyone she met had a reason to kill her. Everyone except her devoted number two. I played that role so well, don't you think? I mean she literally asked me to bring her the poison!" Her voice turned high pitched in a cruel imitation of the late witch. " 'Oh Margaret I could just go for a cream tea, you know just how I like it, would you mind? Honey then cream.' Pah, of course I knew how she liked it, she always invited me over for tea and then asked me to make it! I was the only one she trusted. The stupid bitch. And she always said my honey was the only honey she'd ever eat. She was right about that! She always had to be right about everything!"

"But how?"

Margaret face morphed into a sly smile. "Ah, not so clever then, are you? I had to make sure I prepared the scones, but they had to be the same ones you were serving so the police wouldn't suspect me. So, I knocked the plate over and took one when I helped pick them back up. Poor clumsy Margaret."

"Well, it's over now." Fi took a step towards the witch.

"Over? Oh, I don't think it is…"

Chapter 37

Margaret raised her hands, and her beehives buzzed loudly. Fi took a step back and looked around. Clouds of bees were leaving their hives and massing overhead. Her head snapped back to Margaret. A small smile played on the older witch's lips, sinister in the darkening afternoon light.

"Such a pity you decided to disturb the hives…"

Run! Cressida screamed in Fi's mind and the wyrm dashed under one of the bushes.

Fi grabbed Agatha's arm and ran. The two sisters dodged between the hives as the mega swarm continued to grow. The buzzing grew in volume until it reverberated through their heads. Agatha pushed Fi into a bed of pink rhododendrons by a trailing wisteria. Agatha plunged her hand into the black soil and closed her eyes. The bees' tune changed to an angry whine.

Vines spread from the wisteria and grew around the witches, encircling them in a living cage. Agatha pressed her lips together, and the vines twined thickly around each other, blocking off the rest of the garden. Hail rained down on their sanctuary as the storm broke. A nasty buzzing punctuated the drumming of the ice. Fi realised it wasn't hail. The pattering she could hear was the sound of the bees throwing themselves against the vines.

The buzzing intensified. It was inside the vines.

"Ouch!" Fi flicked the dying body of the bee that had stung her to the ground and focused on the small creatures flying inside the barrier Agatha had created. One dived for her face, and she ducked to one side. She shrugged off her trench coat and flailed it around to swat bees as best she could in the cramped space. She spotted a patch of grey sky.

"Agatha!" Fi shouted, pointing at the small hole the bees were getting through.

Agatha nodded, and the vines moved under her control to completely block them in. Fi swatted the remaining bees with two swipes of her trench coat. Fi felt a pang of regret for the tiny creatures as they lay on the floor.

"Kill them." Agatha hissed. Fi turned to her sister, frowning. "She's controlling the bees. We can't have them in here with us."

As if Agatha's words inspired it, one bee wrenched itself into the air and stung Fi on the neck. The tech witch swore and swatted it away. The pain took the sting out of making sure the rest of the insects were dead.

"We're trapped," Agatha stated the obvious.

"How long can you keep this up?"

"Depends if all she throws at us is bees…"

Fi swore again. More bees crept between gaps in the tangled vines. She gathered her own power to her hands and waited. She had one shot, maybe two. If she could control her power. Big if. Agatha swore as several of the swarm stung her. The vines crinkled at the lack of concentration before the nature witch focused her power.

Fi cursed. Her magic wasn't enough to take out a swarm of bees. But she didn't need to take out the bees. Just the killer witch controlling them. Thunder crashed over the intense buzzing. An idea flitted into Fi's head.

"Do you think you could make a tree grow?"

Agatha looked at her sister, puzzled. "Not while I'm keeping this up. I can feel the bees pressing against the vines. If I stop, they'll be on us in seconds. Do you know how many stings it takes for a person to die from bee venom?"

Fi shook her head.

"Neither do I, and I don't want to find out!"

Fi snorted at her sister's gallows humour. "I think I've got a plan…"

Chapter 38

Fi nodded to her sister. Agatha let the vines drop. The swarm clustered about them. Fi siphoned enough of her electricity to charge the air around the two sisters. The air felt thick and close. Bees crackled as they connected with the electric charge. Burning filled Fi's nostrils. Agatha forced the plants around them upwards, swaying vines and leaves to bat the bees back further.

Fi stepped forward.

"What are you doing to my bees?" Margaret's voice was hysterical.

"You're doing this to them, Margaret. Stop now and let us help you."

"Help me?! You'll turn me into the police and then it'll be the rest of my life at his majesty's pleasure. I don't think so!"

The bees redoubled their efforts to get at the two witches. The air fizzed as the small insects launched themselves into the electrical field.

"Nooooo!" Margaret made a complicated movement with her hands and the bees lifted up above them, hovering a foot over their heads. The swarm swirled in the muggy air, building up speed. The heat of it pressed down on Fi. If the entire mass of bees hit them at once, she wasn't sure her electric field would hold.

She reached out and up with her power, trying to sense the air. The air particles popped with charge. She felt like she could sense every bee and their tiny movements filled with a positive charge from the friction of flying. If only they weren't under Margaret's control, maybe she could contact them somehow. But there was no time for that. Her hair stood on end as the static charge grew. Any minute now…

She dropped her shield. Agatha's vines continued to thwack at the insects, but they soon realised they could get through and swirled down to attack the sisters.

"Ow! I can't keep this up! We need to do it soon!" Agatha called from behind her. Fi heard her sister fall to the ground. Fi kept her eyes on Margaret. She felt the air fill with electric potential.

"Now!"

Agatha forced her power through the soil. She found a seed, so full of potential, waiting for Spring. She plunged her energy into it, forcing it to grow now. A sprout pushed out of the ground. The trunk widened, and it was a sapling, then a young tree still reaching upwards towards the sky.

Leaves unfurled behind Margaret. The killer heard nothing over the intense buzzing trill of the millions of bees in the sky, waiting for the command to descend. Agatha poured all of her magic into the growing tree, then panted, waiting for her sister to act.

Fi ran towards the beekeeper. Margaret's mouth hung open in surprise before her eyes glinted with malice. Fi let her power unfurl up into the dark sky. She wasn't sure of her power, but she was sure about lightning. Fi eyed the tree behind Margaret. Perfect. Lightning preferred the easiest path.

The bees plunged into her. She ignored the needle like pain of stings connecting with her hands and face. A sudden heat flared at her legs. She looked down. Cressida was there, breathing fire at the bees, giving Fi some protection as they veered to avoid the flames. Fi wanted to ask about the fire, but she had to focus. She sent all he power and will into the sky. She had one shot at this.

The gathering storm exploded above them. The sky crackled. Lightning was everywhere. It followed the path Fi had made and more, fracturing into the tree behind the beekeeper. The newly grown tree splintered into pieces with a bang. The bungalow shook.

Light hung in the air, as if time had slowed and the storm dumped everything it had in one burst. Margaret screamed. The bolt exploded through the tree into her. She fell to the ground.

The bees' angry whine dulled to a more natural hum. Fi collapsed to the floor. Thunder rumbled above her. The sky cleared. It was preternaturally calm.

The bees flew up into the blue sky. Fi watched the super swarm flee over the fields, freed from Margaret's influence. Fi's senses were heightened, as if her body was trying to absorb every single detail. She fancied she could see every individual insect as it moved in the swarm and their energy had changed; they felt more relaxed now Margaret wasn't controlling them. Many minds working as one. Her last thought was that she had probably destroyed her new phone.

Don't you leave me as well!

The last thing she felt was a rough tongue licking her face.

Chapter 39

They could have made it gold.

"Stop grumbling! A brass plaque is a fine memorial," Fi whispered, trying not to sound like she was talking to herself.

It's barely big enough to fit her name on it, let alone all her accomplishments.

Fi turned her snort of laughter into a cough. "I think they're just getting her name on it. At least she's getting some sort of memorial."

The wyrm chuntered to herself and pushed forward to get a spot near the front of the small crowd. She placed herself near Nell's feet. As a fellow chair of the WWWI, the senior witch had been designated to unveil the plaque. The irony had been lost on nobody, but Nell did her best not to grind her teeth as she gave a short speech praising the deceased witch. Privately, she had hoped that she would be the first witch in the tri-village area to be so commemorated after her work at Avalon, but she'd been pipped to the posthumous.

Fi smiled at her mother's discomfort. Nell had been moaning all week, ever since the National Chair of the WWWI had contacted her with the news that there was to be a plaque. Fi caught Liv's eye across the other side of the crowd and nodded. Her friend smiled back at her. She took that as an invitation to walk over.

"Hey."

"Hey, I like the new look."

Fi smoothed a hand through her white hair. A symptom of using so much power, or at least that's what Madam Mim and Nell thought. Fi gave her friend an uncertain grin. She was still getting used to her new locks, "I dunno, it's a bit grown up for me."

"How are you feeling?"

Fi shrugged, "Oh, you know, fine, considering I had enough bee poison in me to kill me."

"You were lucky Madam Mim was still around."

Fi nodded. She had been lucky. She had passed out, but Agatha had filled her in on the details. Effie had had a vision about the showdown and persuaded Madam Mim to investigate when the police ignored her.

Margaret was dead, killed by a lightning strike, it was assumed. Although they hadn't found her body, just a pile of ash near a dead tree. There was much talk among the Cotswold witches about what on earth she had been doing tending her hives when a storm was coming, and under a tree no less.

The police, when they had finally turned up, found enough oleander honey to poison an entire branch of the WWWI, so Fi had been cleared. Rumours rushed around the Cotswolds about what she was going to do with so much deadly honey.

And Cressida had continued lick and prod Fi to try to bring her to consciousness.

Madam Mim had poured enough healing magic into Fi's body to counteract the venom. It should have been a satisfying ending. Except Fi's thoughts kept turning to Margaret's face, and the sickening smell of charred flesh. Her power had hurt someone. Again. Even if the old witch had tried to kill her, Fi wondered if she could have found another way.

"And how's it going now you're back with your mum?" Liv's question pulled Fi out of her spiralling thoughts.

Fi grimaced. "It's not too bad really. Mum's been great, and it really is the only solution until I find a new job."

Liv place a sympathetic hand on Fi's arm. "Don't force yourself. You've just been through a significant trauma, and you've got a lot to process."

Fi nodded then she squared her shoulders and met Liv's eyes. "Look, I'm really sorry about…I shouldn't have asked…"

Liv raised her hand. "It's forgotten. I'm just glad you're OK, both of you."

Fi looked over her shoulder, following Liv's gaze. Agatha approached, "How are you feeling?"

"Good. Thank you. For everything." Fi reached out and gave her sister an awkward pat on the arm.

"What are big sisters for?"

"Hey, did they ever catch the pumpkin?"

Agatha shook her head wryly. "No. It was last seen heading across the stone circle. I don't think it will cause any trouble, I'm sure it just wants a nice shady and sunny place to put down roots."

"I still don't understand how it's alive…" Liv eyed the sisters.

Agatha shrugged. "No one's really sure, but Madam Mim's best guess is that the huge discharge of electric and growth magic granted the pumpkin some sort of animation. Either that or it was destroyed by the overwhelming magical energies and people made up the sightings. Either way, it's a pumpkin, nothing to worry about."

Liv turned away to speak to Sita. Effie wandered over.

"Something wicked is coming, I can feel it," she said without preamble. The hairs on Fi's neck rose with a sense of foreboding.

"What do you mean?"

"I have to prepare." Effie turned to leave.

Agatha and Fi exchanged a look. "Probably just one of her funny turns," Agatha whispered."

"I heard that! And I'll have you know that my feelings are never wrong." Effie prodded a bony finger into Agatha's chest. "I wasn't wrong about the Kennedy assassination and that was before your time, missy!"

"Sorry, Effie. Can we help at all?"

The nonagenarian scowled and backed off. "No, this is something I have to face myself."

Effie walked away and Agatha rubbed the spot where Effie had poked her. "For such a small lady, she's surprisingly strong," she said when Effie was out of ear shot.

Fi took the chance to take something out of her pocket. She shoved it into Agatha's hand.

Agatha looked down. "What's this?"

Fi shrugged. Agatha unravelled the paper and recognised the cheque. Her eyes widened and she stared at Fi.

"I thought it was about time I started thinking about someone else. Use it to take Bea to Disneyland or something. Goddess knows you could use a holiday."

Agatha smiled and pulled her sister into a hug. "You're un-bee-lievable, you know that?"

"You'd better bee-lieve it."

Fi's phone rang. She extricated herself from her sister's embrace and moved away from the crowd to take the call.

"Hello there, this is Haernson's Dragon Ranch, I'm calling to arrange a day when we can collect your wyrm."

"Oh, right."

"We can be with you on Thursday if that works? About three o'clock?"

"Oh right…" Fi looked over at the small wyrm staring forlornly up at the brass plaque. Maybe it would be nice to have some company back at her Mum's house. "Well, the thing is…I think I've changed my mind."

"You mean about the collection day? I could do the Friday if you prefer."

"No, I mean about giving her up. I think I'd rather she stayed."

"Wonderful! Well now, that's lovely to hear. Did I mention we run an owner's course? Accommodation and food included, would you like the details?"

Fi smiled. "I think I would."

She hung up and nearly tripped over Cressida, who had appeared at her feet.

So, you're not sending me away?

Fi bent down and scratched the small wyrm under her chin. "Guess we're a team now."

Cressida flicked her tail. *Glad to see you've come to your senses.*

Epilogue

Fi gripped her seat as the taxi bumped along the country road.

"Good job you booked me from the station. The GPS takes you to the middle of nowhere, but I know my way to the Dragon Ranch. Dylan and Owain are lovely, they always bring the best drinks along to our town's Christmas party. Are you staying long?"

"Just for a week," Fi said through gritted teeth, wishing the driver would keep his eyes on the road instead of twisting round to talk to her.

Cressida stretched up to put her front feet on the window, then jumped down and paced the length of the footwell before returning to her sentry pose at the window. The small wyrm vibrated with excitement.

We're nearly there!

"I don't know how you can see anything with all this rain," Fi grumbled.

"Oh, it's just a bit of drizzle, a traditional Welsh welcome for you! You should have been here last year; I swear it rained from October through to March!"

"I can believe it," Fi mumbled under her breath as she stared out of the window. The 'drizzle' pelted the window hard and the taxi's windscreen wipers moved back and forth at breakneck speed, trying to clear the view. A flash of lightning illuminated a swinging sign of a dragon twisted around an Anvil. Fi just had time to make out the words: Haernson's Dragon Ranch.

Cressida scratched at the window, desperate to get out.

"Stop it! I'm not paying for any claw damage!" Fi hissed, hoping the driver hadn't noticed.

The driver pulled up as close to the large stone cottage as he could, and Fi pressed some notes into his hand for the fare.

"Say hi to Owain and Dylan for me!" He waited politely for her to get out. Fi grabbed her suitcase and the wyrm's lead and opened the door. She stepped into a puddle that could almost be called a pond. She swore. Why had she worn her converse trainers to rural Wales?

She slammed the taxi door behind her as she squelched forward. Cressida pulled on the lead. It slipped out of Fi's hand and trailed along behind the golden wyrm as she bounded towards the farmhouse. She scratched at the door.

Fi blinked, trying to see through the driving rain and mounted the couple of steps to the front door. She lifted her hand to knock but the door opened before her knuckles connected with the wood.

"Hello, hello, and who's this then? A thoroughbred, is it? Aren't you gorgeous?" The broad bearded dwarf bent down to scratch the golden wyrm under her chin. Cressida practically purred. Fi stared at the top of his head. His rusty brown hair was pulled back into a thick queue.

Another dwarf appeared behind the first, rubbing flour covered hands on his apron. The slogan on it read 'A dragon is for life, not just for Christmas'. "Owain, our guest is soaked! Move aside and let her in!"

The first dwarf picked up Cressida easily and stepped aside. "Sorry, come in, come in. I'll just put the kettle on, shall I?"

Fi stepped inside, trying not to stare at the dwarf's face. He had a large pink burn on one cheek and one eyebrow was missing. She wiped the water from her eyes and focused on the tall grandfather clock in the hall and stood, dripping on the mat in the entryway. The first dwarf didn't notice her awkwardness and headed through a door to the right. Fi realised that the other dwarf was waiting politely. "Do you have coffee?"

The second dwarf laughed, "We've got Goblin Blend if you like the strong stuff or instant."

"Goblin Blend please."

"I'll let Owain know. I'm Dylan," he extended his hand and took hers. His skin was warm and rough against hers. He shook her small, damp hand thoroughly as he continued, "You'll be staying in the old barn for the week." He must have picked up on Fi's horrified expression because he laughed heartily, "Don't worry, it's been converted into rooms. You won't be sleeping on the hay! But we've fireproofed all the outbuildings so you can stay there with your wyrm and get some quality bonding time in between the lessons. Owain'll show you there now."

Fi looked back at the door. "Now? It's tipping it down!"

Another loud laugh. "Just a bit of rain, and it's not like you'll get any wetter!" He had a point. "There's wet weather gear in your room. When you've changed into something dry, come back over and you can meet the others for dinner. Owain!"

His shout drew the other dwarf from the kitchen. Cressida was curled around his neck, making happy little growls. He passed a mug of coffee to Fi with a broad grin.

Owain pulled his own raincoat and waterproof trousers on and opened the door. He took Fi's suitcase and strode happily into the rain. Fi sighed and followed behind. It was a short but muddy journey to the nearest looming outbuilding. Fi could just about make out five doors in the side of the building. Owain wrenched open one and stepped inside. He fumbled in the dark for a moment before finding the light switch. Fi entered gratefully and stepped inside.

"Okey dokey, you've got the wyrm's bed there by the radiator, nice and cosy, and we've got the best Welsh coal for her in the food dish. That's obviously your bed there and your protective gear is in the wardrobe. It doubles as wet weather gear, so doubly handy! Shower room's through that door over there. If you need anything, just come over to the farmhouse and ask. Dinner's ready, so come over as soon as your ready." He held out his arm, and Cressida gracefully descended and raced to her bed. "Leave the wyrm here for this evening. Dylan likes to have the first evening with just the owners and it'll do her good to get settled in. See you in a bit." With that, he headed back out into the rain.

Fi stared after him, her head reeling. She took a sip of her coffee, made drinking temperature by the rain that had dropped into the mug on the way over. What she really wanted was a shower, but he had said everyone was waiting for her so instead, she stripped out of her wet things and towelled herself off with the biggest, fluffiest towel she could find. Once she was dry, she selected the smartest clothes she'd brought with her and tugged the heavy overalls that were made of some sort of tough leather over the top. She noticed the boots in the wardrobe too and slipped them on. Suitably covered, she pulled up the hood and went to the door.

Rather you than me. Cressida opened one lazy eye.

"Thanks for the support." Fi shook her head at the wyrm before she pulled on the door and stepped outside.

She ran the short distance to the farmhouse as quickly as she could in the bulky overclothes and thick-soled boots. Panting, she knocked loudly on the door. Dylan opened it with a large smile on his face. He ushered her in and instructed her to hang her things on one of the pegs lining the wall. Once she had peeled herself out of the protective clothing, he led her to the dining room. Three other faces looked at her expectantly as she entered. She ran her hand through her hair, trying to smooth it down and waved. She sank into an empty seat, put her phone on the table and stared self-consciously at the thick ceramic plate in front of her.

Owain strode into the room, a small green wyrm sitting on his shoulder, making him look like some sort of pirate. "Ah, here you are. Now we can start!" He poured everyone a large glass of ruby red wine and raised his up.

"Welcome to the Dragon Ranch wyrm handler's beginner's training programme." He took a deep drink that drained half his glass. Fi and the others sipped theirs at the toast. She didn't like wine, but she didn't want to be rude so forced herself to have one taste before switching to water. It seemed rude to ask for a diet coke. Owain wiped his mouth with the back of his hand and carried on.

"Firstly, thank you all for coming. I know that owning a wyrm can be rewarding, but it can also be a challenge. That's why you're here, to learn how to care for them and meet their needs and how to train them so they aren't a social menace." He laughed at his own poor joke.

"Of course, it's no joke really. The government is thinking about cracking down on wyrm ownership so it's important that these animals are properly trained and don't injure anyone else.

"Dylan and I founded this ranch over fifty years ago to care for these special creatures and it means so much that you've chosen us to help you," a tear welled up in one of his brown eyes and the wyrm on his shoulder nuzzled his singed beard affectionately. He tickled the wyrm's head and looked around the room.

"This course is focused on your relationship with your wyrm so while we'll be working as a group, you won't handle each other's animals. The one other rule I have is that this is a safe space and there is no judgement. If you're happy with that and are willing to learn, then we'll have a productive time. Now tonight is about us getting to know each other. So, while Dylan brings out the excellent meal he's prepared, why don't you all introduce yourselves and tell us why you're here?"

There was a pause as Dylan entered, his beard slicked into neat plaits. He laid down two enormous crockery pots filled with a hearty stew, then retreated into the kitchen and returned with bread rolls the size of Fi's head. He passed the wicker basket of rolls around before spooning up the stew. Fi closed her eyes and breathed in the rich aroma of the stew. She hadn't realised how hungry she was.

"Tuck in, before it gets cold," Dylan motioned as he took a bite out of his own hunk of bread.

The small green wyrm darted across the table and sank his teeth into one of the rolls.

"Owain!"

"Get down, you silly wyrm," Owain flapped a hand towards the wyrm. Sharptooth skittered off the table, picking the spot next to Fi to jump down and run off.

"Sorry about that, he can get a little excitable. Go on, tell us about yourself," Owain urged one of the participants. A man in his fifties with grey hair, round spectacles and a sleeveless knitted jumper over a white shirt. The man coughed and took another sip of wine to compose himself.

"I'm Clint and this is my wife Shirley," his wife waved, her Farrah Fawcett hairdo shaking at her exuberance. "We're looking after our daughter's wyrm while she's on secondment in Singapore…"

"It's a big promotion for her!" Shirley added, "We're so proud! And it's such a prestigious firm, she's done so well. Sorry, carry on, dear."

"Anyway, she left us with this creature…"

"She said it would be good for us now we're retired. Clint used to run our local bank branch until it got shut down. Sorry, carry on, dear."

"So now we're looking after it for twelve months and it's already burned our sofa…"

"Singed the arm! Now it's completely black! We were lucky it didn't burn the house down, but we got a terrible fright I tell you. Sorry, carry on, dear."

"So, we're here to get some tips on how to make it behave, because apparently giving the thing away isn't an option."

"No, she loves it so much! But it's such a big upheaval for the poor thing and the airline's have such strict rules about animals. So, we're taking care of the little thing," Shirley beamed at everyone.

Owain blinked as if he were shell-shocked. "Thank you for sharing. Now how about you?"

A younger man in his twenties leaned forward and smiled, punctuating the air with his fork as he spoke. "Hi everyone, great to meet you! I'm Theo. My other half really wants a baby. We've wanted one for forever, I suppose that's why we got Pim really. But now she's pregnant but little Pim, our wyrm, he's not really the best behaved and we're worried how he'll react to the baby so I'm here to train him up."

The dwarves shared a look and Dylan looked like he might say something, but Owain turned to Fi and nodded.

"Uh, hi there," she forced herself not to touch her hair, "I'm Fi and I sort of inherited a wyrm, so that's why I'm here." The others looked at her, expecting more. "Uh, I guess we don't really get on and Cressida, that's her name, broke a lot of my stuff so yeah…hoping to get some tips this week."

Everyone nodded and the focus shifted from the witch to the delicious food. Fi concentrated on chewing the tender lamb, which practically melted in her mouth.

"So, what is it you do?" Theo asked Fi between mouthfuls.

Fi swallowed, "Uh, I'm in between jobs right now."

"Cool, I'm a project manager."

"Oh, that's lovely. Ciara, that's our daughter, she manages portfolios, always working late."

Fi let the conversation wash over her, not really noticing they had moved to dessert until Dylan brandished a large fruit cake. She reached for her phone to take a picture then frowned. It wasn't next to her plate, odd, but she must have left it back in her room.

"That looks amazing!" cooed Shirley as the dwarf cut them each an enormous slice and then poured thick cream over the top.

Fi took a spoonful. The fumes coming off it almost overwhelmed her. Dylan chuckled, "It's my mother's recipe, God love her. She always says the alcohol's the best part."

Fi ate it slowly, savouring the plump raisins. Clint even asked for seconds. After they'd finished, Owain poured them all some mead for a nightcap and regaled them with stories about previous courses. After an hour of nightcaps, Dylan carefully took his husband's glass away from him.

Owain took the hint. "Right, I suppose it's bedtime."

Fi stood up, swaying slightly. She hadn't even drunk the mead; what had been in that cake? She wondered dazedly if the room was spinning as the dwarf continued; "Tomorrow, the real work begins!"

If you want to find out how the rest of the stay at the Dragon Ranch went, sign up to my mailing list at www.gemmaclatworthy.com for a free short story.

Thank you for reading book one in the Omensford series. If you enjoyed this book, you can get a free prequel to my Rise of Dragons series and join the conversation at Gemma's book wyrms or read along with all my books before they're published on patreon.

As an independent author, your reviews help me decide which series to keep going so please do leave one for Bedsocks & Broomsticks and if you enjoyed this book try, Crystal Balls & Cream Teas, book two in the Omensford series.

Books in the Omensford series:

Bedsocks & Broomsticks

Crystal Balls & Cream Teas [coming soon]

Demons & Donkeys [coming soon]

Books in the Rise of Dragons series:

Awakening

Solstice of Dragons

Equinox Betrayal

Darkest Deception

Attack on Avalon

Fated Bloodlines

Thank You

A special thank you to my amazing patreon: Emma Ward who always supports me.

If you want to support Gemma, you can find her on patreon for exclusive first reads of new stories.

You can also join her newsletter for a free prequel to her Rise of Dragons series and follow Gemma on www.instagram.com/gemmaclatworthy, www.facebook.com/gemmaclatworthy or join the reader's group Gemma's book wyrms.

Other Books by G Clatworthy

Books in the Rise of the Dragons series:

Awakening

Solstice of Dragons

Equinox Betrayal

Darkest Deception

Attack on Avalon

Fated Bloodlines

Books in the Omensford series (set in the Rise of Dragons universe):

Bedsocks and Broomsticks

Cream Teas and Crystal Balls

Demons and Donkeys

Children's Books

The Child Who series:

The Girl Who Lost Her Listening Ears

The Boy Who Lost His Listening Ears

The Girl Who Dreamed of Sleep

The Boy Who Dreamed of Sleep

Nanny Pastry series:

Nanny Pastry and the Nimble Ninjabread Man

Other books:

Coronavirus in the words of children

About the Author

Gemma started writing during the 2020 lockdown and loves fantasy fiction and dragons in particular. She lives in Wiltshire with her family and two cats and also enjoys crafts of all kinds. You can see all her writing on patreon. Join the conversation at Gemma's book wyrms readers' group on Facebook.

She also writes children's books. You can find out more on her website www.gemmaclatworthy.com or follow her on Instagram (www.instagram.com/gemmaclatworthy) or Facebook (www.facebook.com/gemmaclatworthy).